THE
CHRISTMAS
WISH

ALSO BY RICHARD SIDDOWAY

Twelve Tales of Christmas
Mom and Other Great Women I Have Known
Habits of the Heart

THE CHRISTMAS WISH

BY

RICHARD SIDDOWAY

HARMONY BOOKS
NEW YORK

Published by Harmony Books, a division of Crown Publishers, Inc.,
201 East 50th Street, New York, New York 10022.
Member of the Crown Publishing Group.

Originally published in a different format by Bookcraft, Inc., in 1995.
Copyright © 1995 by Richard M. Siddoway.

Random House, Inc., New York, Toronto, London, Sydney, Auckland
www.randomhouse.com

HARMONY and colophon are trademarks of Crown Publishers, Inc.

Printed in the United States of America

DESIGN BY MAGGIE HINDERS

Library of Congress Cataloging-in-Publication Data
Siddoway, Richard M.
The Christmas wish / by Richard Siddoway. — 1st ed.
I. Grandfathers—Fiction. 2. Young men—Fiction. I. Title.
[PS3569.I29C48   1998]   98-27385
813'.54—dc21   CIP

ISBN 0-609-60414-7

10 9 8 7 6 5 4 3 2 1

Revised Edition

To Janice

The house is warm, good cheer abounds.
The heart of Christmas is all around.
The children sing, their voices sweet,
The candles are lit, such rosy heat,
My heart is full, my eyes aglow,
For those here with me and those I cannot know.
May peace be ours, may peace be theirs,
Let us remember all mankind in our Christmas prayers.

ANONYMOUS

THE CHRISTMAS WISH

1

THE SILVER JAGUAR XJ6 SENT PINWHEELS OF RED AND GOLD LEAVES INTO THE AUTUMN TWILIGHT AS WILL MARTIN LEFT THE INTERSTATE AND APPROACHED THE town of his birth. As always a feeling of melancholy enveloped him as he drove down the two-lane highway lined with century-old crimson maples whose boughs intertwined and formed a shadowy tunnel across the road. The powerful engine hummed as he maneuvered the gentle twists and turns that led to the town. Will fished the cellular phone from his inside coat pocket and punched in a number.

"Mick," he said into the phone. "I'm sorry I'm late. I was hoping you'd still be at your shop." He smiled at the reply. "I'm less than five minutes away. Thanks." He punched the *end* button on the phone and returned it to his pocket.

The last vestiges of sunlight brushed the tops of the trees in the town square as he slid the Jaguar to the curb in front of Mick's Flower Shop. He hopped out and hurried into the shop. Mick sat behind the cash register counting the day's receipts. He looked up as he entered the store. "Afternoon, Will. It was nice of you to call, but I figured you'd still want the bouquet you ordered. I wasn't going anywhere until you arrived."

Will smiled as the white-haired old man rose from his chair and made his way to the walk-in cooler in the back of the shop. He emerged a few moments later holding a dozen yellow roses. "This okay, Will?" He held the bouquet lovingly in his hands. "Or should I call you Mr. Martin now that you're running the agency?" Mick's eyes crinkled up at Will.

" 'Will' will be fine," he replied, with a smile of his own. "The flowers look great, Mick. How much do I owe you?"

"Hmm, I suppose I ought to give you the same price I gave your grandfather. After all, I don't suppose I'd be in business if it weren't for him." Will lifted a quizzical eyebrow. "But that's another story for another day. Ten dollars."

"Are you sure? That seems awfully reasonable. Especially when I kept you open on Thanksgiving Day."

"Yup, ten dollars. That's the Martin price, including tax." The old man smiled. Will handed him a ten-dollar bill. "Thanks, Mick, I'd like to hear that story some time." He took the roses and raced back to the car. He glanced at his watch as the powerful engine pulled the car from the curb. *If I can make it to Julia's in five minutes, I'll be on time,* he thought. He steered through the light traffic around the town square and hurried down Olive Street to the new condominiums that had sprung up on the edge of town. He slid into a parking spot and hurried up the steps to Julia's front door.

Inside, Julia Welsch admired herself in the hall mirror. The dark red suit she wore accentuated her honey-blond hair. She leaned close to the mirror and inspected her face. Quickly she reached into her bag and applied a fresh dab of color to her lips. The grandfather clock chimed melodiously, as the doorbell rang. *Well, he's on time,* she smiled, *that's a first.* She picked up her dark green overcoat, opened the door, and accepted Will's kiss on the cheek.

"You look gorgeous," he said as he took her arm and led her to the waiting car.

"You don't look so bad yourself," she replied, sinking into the leather seat. *Maybe things are moving along at last,* Julia thought, *at least he's finally taking me home to meet his grandmother.*

Will glanced at the woman sitting next to him. *I'm a lucky guy. I hope Gram approves of her.* He smiled at Julia as she examined herself in the mirror set in the sun visor. The Jaguar sped across town. Will turned into the circular drive in front of a two-story brick home bounded by neatly trimmed hedges. A covered porch ran the width of the house. The manicured lawn was covered with autumn leaves. The smell of wood smoke hung in the air as Will helped Julia from the car. Immediately the front door flew open and Ruth Martin stepped onto the porch. She was wearing a dark blue dress that set off her silver hair. Although seventy-five years of age, she looked ten years younger. Will hugged her, handed her the roses, and kissed her cheek. "Gram, this is Julia Welsch." Ruth Martin smiled broadly and held Julia's hands in hers as she looked into the young woman's clear blue eyes.

"Come in, come in," she said, as she led them into the foyer of her home. "Will, it's so good to have you home for the holidays this year."

"It's good to be here."

"Dinner's ready. Why don't you get Miss Welsch seated in the dining room and then help me bring in the food from the kitchen."

Will led Julia through the living room, through the French doors, and into the dining room. The table was set with the pale ivory linen cloth and the crystal he knew would be there. This meal always began the holiday season for the Martin family, and the menu never varied. He pulled out a chair for Julia. "I'll be right back," he whispered as she took her seat.

Julia inspected the dining room while she waited. The Spode china reflected her perfect face as she gazed across the room at the painting of Warren Martin hanging on the wall above the sideboard. Two elegant silver candelabra bracketed the picture. Julia turned to find a similar painting of Ruth Martin on the wall behind her. She examined the silverware and noticed that the handle of each knife was engraved with the family crest. She thought of the handsome man helping his grandmother in the kitchen and smiled a deep, satisfied smile. *Thirty-two years is long enough for him to be single.*

The kitchen door swung open and Will appeared, his cheeks flushed from the steaming, roasted turkey he carried. He placed it on the table as his grandmother appeared balancing a bowl of mashed potatoes in one hand and cranberry jelly in the other. Quickly the rest of the food was retrieved from the kitchen.

"Will, you're the man of the house now. Please say a blessing on the food, and thank the Lord for all the good things He's given us this year." She placed the vase of yellow roses in the middle of the table and quietly bowed her head.

Will cleared his throat and offered a prayer of thanksgiving. When he finished, he looked at his grandmother's face and saw the hint of a tear in her eye. He began to carve the turkey.

They chatted as they ate, speaking companionably about family and work and cultural interests, punctuated by compliments to Ruth about the feast they were enjoying. As they were finishing their pumpkin pie, Julia said, "Mrs. Martin, did you know that I'm in charge of the Country Club Christmas Ball this year?"

"Oh, how nice. Is this your first time?" Ruth asked.

"Yes, and I've had such great support from the community. Everyone seems so excited about the dance. It's a chance to put on our Christmas finery and help support the development of a new children's wing at the hospital. I'm delighted to be a part of it."

"I'm sure you are," Ruth said, smiling.

"We've asked for RSVPs, you know. The caterers just have to have some idea of the number of people they're going to serve. I mean, you just couldn't have them run out of food, now, could you?" Julia asked with a knowing look in Ruth's direction. "Will," she continued, as she lowered her eyes and looked at him, "I haven't seen your RSVP yet, but I'm sure it's not necessary. I'm certain I'm going to make everyone else jealous with the handsomest man in town at my side."

Will glanced at his grandmother, an embarrassed look on his face.

"What about you, Mrs. Martin. Will you be joining us at the ball?" Julia beamed in her direction.

A shadow crossed Ruth Martin's face. "I haven't made up my mind. I'm not sure I'm ready to get back into the social whirl quite yet."

"But it will be *the* event of the season," persisted Julia. "You really must come."

"Thank you for your kind invitation," Ruth replied quietly. "I'll just have to see how I feel."

The smile hardened on Julia's face. "I'll put you down as a yes. The evening just won't be complete without you." In the uncomfortable silence that followed, Julia turned to Will. "Guess who called me today."

Will shook his head. "I'm sure I can't imagine."

"Angela Davidson," Julia gushed. A bewildered look crossed Will's face. "She invited us to go skating with her family when we're in New York next month." Julia's eyes sparkled with anticipation. "The Christmas tree at Rockefeller Center," she wrapped her arms around herself. "It has to be the center of Christmas in New York. The skating rink is crowded, but Angela says it's always a part of the Davidson Christmas tradition."

"That's great," Will murmured, "sounds like a Kodak moment to me." He looked at his grandmother, who was gazing longingly at the picture of Warren Martin on the wall behind Will. "Julia," he said, "have I ever told you about the Christmas traditions I grew up with in this house?"

"I don't think so," she replied.

"Well, much of it centered on Christmas Eve." Ruth Martin smiled fondly at Will as he spoke. "It might seem silly—I mean, so many people start shopping the day after

Thanksgiving—but we always waited until Christmas Eve, that was our shopping day. Gram would take me downtown with the money I'd earned. Some people think everything is a little shopworn by Christmas Eve, but to me it seemed just the opposite. Nowadays the stores close early, but then they all stayed open until really late."

"Actually, it was only eight o'clock, Will," Gram interrupted. "But when you were a boy, that was late for you."

"At least they haven't changed the town square," Will continued. "It was always decked out for the holidays. There were lights everywhere. People running around doing their shopping. The windows of the stores all decorated. Simpson's clothing store had an animated Santa Claus that I particularly loved. Church bells played carols in the cold, vibrant air and carolers sang near the Nativity scene in the middle of the square." He closed his eyes, remembering. "We'd shop until all of the stores closed and then we'd hurry home to wrap presents. The crowning event was when we'd help Grandpa decorate the Christmas tree." His voice had taken on an edge of melancholy. "I don't think I'll ever forget those evenings." Will looked at his grandmother. She was smiling through the tears that moistened her eyes.

Julia picked absently at a piece of pie crust that remained on her plate. "It sounds wonderful, Will. I guess I don't have those kinds of memories. My mom and dad separated when I was two . . . I, well, it sounds wonderful."

"It was. Of course the hardest part was buying a gift for Gram and hiding it from her till we got home and I could get it wrapped." Will snapped his fingers. "That reminds me, Gram, what do you want for Christmas this year? I hate to break a tradition, but I'm not going to leave it until Christmas Eve this year, if I can help it."

Ruth Martin shook her head. "Don't be silly, just having you home from New York is more than enough."

"You're not getting off that easy. There must be something."

"Will, when you get to be my age there isn't much you want, and there's very, very little you need."

"Gram, I insist. I'd rather get you something you'd like instead of some useless doodad."

Ruth Martin's slender fingers traced the filigreed swirls on the water goblet in front of her. She paused for a moment, then said, "Maybe there is one thing, Will. Excuse me a moment." She rose quietly from her place at the head of the table and left the room.

"What's up?" Julia whispered, looking across the table at Will.

He shrugged his shoulders. The room grew quiet, as they listened to the ticking of the wall clock.

"Will, is your grandmother all right? She doesn't seem to be quite with it, do you know what I mean? She's . . . oh, I don't know, sort of up one minute and down the next."

A frown creased Will's brow. "It's the first Christmas without Grandpa. I'm not sure I can totally appreciate how hard that has been on her, especially a couple who were as close as the two of them were. I've never known a couple who were so connected, so much in tune with each other. And even though he got his wish, it has been really tough on her."

"His wish?" Julia asked, looking puzzled.

"He often said that when he died he wanted to go quickly so that he wasn't a burden on Gram. I guess having a heart attack at the July Fourth celebration in the town square wasn't the best timing, but he was gone by the time they got him to the hospital." Will paused thoughtfully. "I wish you'd known him, Julia. He was one of a kind."

"I wish I had known him, too, but even so there's a time for grief and then you have to get on with your life." Grudgingly Will nodded his head in agreement. "She needs to get out and around. She can't sit in this house day and night." Julia stopped for a moment. "And I was serious when I said she needs to come to the Christmas Ball."

Just then Ruth Martin entered the dining room carrying a small leather-bound journal. She seated herself at the head of the table and placed the book in front of her.

Julia smiled at her warmly. "A book, Mrs. Martin?"

"One of Grandpa's journals," Will said, reaching out to touch the leather lovingly.

"We were married fifty-five years, Julia. And each year one of the Christmas presents we gave each other was one of these journals."

"Fifty-five?" Julia didn't try to hide her amazement.

"Every night when I was a little boy I'd go into his office to kiss him good night and he'd be writing in his journal," said Will.

"I usually wrote in mine in the morning while Warren was away at work. We had an agreement that we'd never look at each other's journals, that way we were free to write our most intimate thoughts. And I kept that promise until Warren died. Since his death I've read some of what he wrote. It has brought back marvelous memories of the times we shared. And it has been interesting to see how differently the two of us viewed the same event."

Will looked across the table at Julia and smiled. She was listening intently to Ruth's narrative.

"And then I found this." Ruth opened the book to a marker she had placed there and began to read. "It's Christmas Eve. Another year has passed. The traditions we all love continue. Ruth and Will have gone shopping. The Christmas tree stands ready to be decorated."

Will smiled at Julia. "See, just as I said."

Ruth Martin cleared her throat and then continued reading. "I do so look forward to this evening. In the meantime, with Ruth gone, it is time for me to visit Lillian."

Will sat forward in his chair. "Lillian? Who's Lillian?"

"I have no idea, Will," Ruth said sadly. "Just no idea."

Will looked around the room, focusing on the painting of his grandfather. "You've got to be kidding."

Slowly Ruth shook her head. "I'm sorry, Will."

Julia looked at the faces around the table. Ruth had closed the book and was staring at the cover. Will was staring at the painting of his grandfather.

"Will, if you really want to get me a Christmas gift, find Lillian."

WILL GUIDED THE JAGUAR INTO THE PARKING SPACE IN FRONT OF JULIA'S CONDO-MINIUM. THE RIDE HOME HAD BEEN SINGU-LARLY QUIET. WILL OPENED THE PASSENGER door and Julia slid out of the car. "Obviously your grand-father had a woman friend. A lot of men do."

"That's impossible," Will said, realizing he sounded defensive.

"That's what they all say. What do you think they were doing together that he couldn't tell your grandmother?"

"Julia, I don't know!" he said emphatically. "But I do know my grandfather. There's just no way he was involved with anyone but Gram."

"Go on thinking what you want," Julia replied as she took his hand. "But your grandfather had everything going for him. He had money. He was good looking. What woman wouldn't want to latch on to him?"

"Julia, he just couldn't have. I mean, I grew up in that house. He was like a father to me. He and Gram were inseparable."

"So you've said. The point is, he was like a father to you. You don't want to believe anything negative about him. But, Will, if you're so sure there wasn't anything going on, then your grandmother's got to feel the same way. Just leave it alone. It's better to let sleeping dogs lie."

"You may be right, but I just told Gram I'd find out and it's the only thing she wants for Christmas. You heard her. And I can't believe that it will be too hard to find this Lillian."

The two of them reached the front door and stood there for a moment. "Want to come in for a while, Will?"

"Thanks, but I'd better not. I've got lots of work to do tomorrow."

Julia slid her hand behind Will's neck. "Thank you for taking me to meet your grandmother. She's quite a woman. The food was wonderful and I appreciate your sharing your Christmas memories with me. I wish I had some of those to fall back on." She shivered in the cool evening air. "How about dinner tomorrow night?"

Will shrugged his shoulders. "I'd like to, but I've really got to get the agency into shape. I've only got a certain amount of time away from my other life in New York City."

Slowly Julia removed her hand from Will's neck. "Can I ask you a question?"

"Sure."

"Are we on the same sheet of music?"

Will looked into Julia's blue eyes. "You're great, you're beautiful, but I'm just overwhelmed. Six months ago I was sitting in my office in New York and my whole world was in order. I'd been made a vice president in my investment firm, with a substantial raise. Then my grandmother called to tell me my grandfather had died and my whole life was thrown into turmoil. When I came home for the funeral I found out he'd left the real estate agency to me. For a while I thought the agency could run itself and then I find it's completely out of touch with the times and needs to be completely revamped. I took a leave of absence from my firm, moved back in with my grandmother, and started try-ing to put things in order, working sixty hours a week— when you dropped into my life."

"You didn't answer my question."

"Julia, I'm not sure exactly what I want right now. I was hoping we could just keep dating a while longer and see how our relationship develops."

"I know what I hope develops," she replied, sliding her hand behind Will's neck again and pulling his head down to hers. He returned the kiss and the embrace.

"Good night, Julia," he said softly, walking slowly down the stairs.

"Good night, Will." She turned and entered her condo. He watched as she closed the door behind her, and he heaved a heavy sigh.

Lillian, he thought, *who in the world is Lillian, where did Grandpa meet her, and what hold did she have over him that he'd spend Christmas Eve with her?* The Jaguar purred quietly through the streets of the town as he returned to his grandmother's home.

When Will opened the hall closet to hang up his coat, he saw his grandfather's hanging on its accustomed peg. Slowly he ran his hand over the soft, old cashmere coat. He could smell the faint odor of his grandfather's aftershave. It was good to be home.

As he started to climb the stairs to his bedroom, he saw his grandmother sitting quietly in her rocking chair by the fireplace. He joined her and found her gazing into the flames. "Oh, Will," she said faintly as she took his hand in hers. "It was good of you to bring Julia here for dinner. It didn't seem quite so lonely." She stroked his hand. "I shouldn't have read the journal to you."

"Of course you should have." He knelt down beside her.

"It's really a private matter, I shouldn't have burdened you with it."

"Grams, it's a family matter. And you and I are all the family we have left. I'm glad you told me." He looked at her hair glowing silver in the firelight. "I can't imagine what you felt when you read that passage."

She stared straight ahead into the flames. "No, I don't think you can imagine, Will. We were together for fifty-five years. I thought we shared everything." She sighed. "Of course Warren didn't talk much about what went on at work. He tried to keep business and family separate. But anything I asked him, he told me about." She fell silent.

"Have you read all of the journals?"

"Oh, heavens no. I've kind of bounced around from one year to another. I'll get reading about some event, like the trip to Yellowstone the year after you came to live with us, then that will remind me of another event and I'll go searching for it. It has all been so fun . . . so exciting, until I read those lines about Lillian."

He got up from his knees and walked to the roll-top desk in the corner of the room. A stack of the journals rested one on top of the other. "Why do you think Grandpa wanted to keep these journals, anyway? I mean, I know you told me at dinner this evening that it was something you each did every year, but why?"

Ruth Martin stopped rocking and rose quietly from her chair. "Your grandfather felt it was very important for each of us to remember the passages that marked our lives, to not forget the little moments or the big ones. Also, I think this was his way of preserving information to pass down to future generations."

"That would make me think that he intended for us to read them."

"That's probably true," Ruth said quietly.

"That means he knew we would read about Lillian!" he exclaimed.

"I...I haven't really thought about that," she said in a whisper.

Will's voice rose with excitement. "Then the real question is not *who* she is, but *why* Grandpa kept her a secret while he was alive."

"But, Will. Warren and I didn't keep secrets. At least, I didn't think so."

3

T HE NEXT MORNING WILL SAT IN HIS
GRANDFATHER'S OFFICE AT MARTIN REAL
ESTATE, THE DESK IN FRONT OF HIM PILED
HIGH WITH STACKS OF PAPERS. *THIS PLACE
looks like it was transported here from the Depression Era,* he thought,
as he sipped a cup of coffee, although he had to admit the
inside of the building had been scrupulously cared for. The
wallpaper above the chair rail was a muted blue stripe and
somehow seemed to fit with the mahogany desks and office
dividers. In fact, there was an ancient elegance about the

building. Will continued to take notes from the file he was inspecting when he heard the front door open. He rose from his chair and started out of his office. Enid Cook was taking off her coat.

"Good morning, Miss Cook."

"Good morning, Mr. Martin. I didn't expect to see you here this morning. I thought it was a holiday weekend."

"It may be for some," he said with a self-deprecating smile, "but others of us have to get the work done."

"Exactly," she replied. "That's why I'm here. I'm trying to get the books closed out for the last quarter." She put her hands on her hips. "Your grandfather expected me to have them ready for him by December first. When will *you* want to look at them? It needs to be soon."

He looked at the late-sixtyish woman who seemed as out of time and place as the office. "I'm sorry, Miss Cook, I guess I didn't know the schedule. Please have my secretary set aside whatever time you think is necessary. She's got me pretty booked up with appointments."

Enid nodded, picked up a handful of folders, and started toward the door. "May I ask where Mr. Henning is?" she sniffed.

"It's a holiday weekend," replied Will.

"I thought he was part of the upper-level management."

Will looked at this anachronistic woman and answered, "He is, but a lot of what needs to be done, I need to do. He'll take over when I go back to New York in January."

"I still think you'd expect him to be here," she huffed. "You're here; where's he?"

Will looked back at the papers in his hands. Enid Cook stood in the open doorway. "Mr. Martin, I hesitate to say this, but I feel I must."

"What's that, Miss Cook?"

"I'm uncomfortable."

"You're uncomfortable?"

"About Martin Real Estate. I don't think you have a complete grasp of how this agency works. I have no idea how you're going to keep track of things here when you return to New York."

"Miss Cook, quite frankly one of the things that bothers me about this agency is that it is so out of touch with the present. It is isolated. Before I go back to New York we will have computers and modems that will allow me to keep my finger on the pulse of this agency from wherever I am in the world. John Henning and I will e-mail each other on a daily basis and I'll make frequent visits. I really don't think there will be any problems."

"Well, frankly, I do. And most of the problems will be because of Mr. Henning. He has no respect for the traditions and reputation enjoyed by this agency. He is totally out of touch with what Martin Real Estate stands for," she said emphatically.

Will placed his hands on the counter that separated the two of them. He was amazed at how quickly this woman could get under his skin. He took a deep breath. "Miss Cook, Mr. Henning graduated with honors from one of the most prestigious business schools in the country. You are absolutely right when you say he doesn't understand this company, and the reason he doesn't is because it is so out-moded. I've hired him to turn this agency around and set it on a leadership path into the next century."

Enid Cook stiffened and rose to her full height as she stared Will Martin straight in the eye. "That, Mr. Martin, is your opinion." She took a step closer and thrust out her chin. "As far as I'm concerned, the Martin Real Estate Agency is fine the way it is."

She snatched her coat from the hook, grabbed the files, and marched out the door. Will stood there shaking his head. The handwriting was on the wall. If he and Henning were going to save this agency, Enid Cook, and maybe several others, would have to go. His musings were interrupted by the telephone. He returned to his desk and pulled up the receiver. "Martin Real Estate, how can I help you?"

"Is that you, Will Martin?"

Will recognized the voice. Sterling Conrad had run another large real estate firm in town. "Yes, it is, Mr. Conrad."

"Just Sterling, my boy. Wondering if you'd like to take advantage of El Niño's gift this year. The golf course is still open. That is if you're not too busy."

Will looked at the pile of papers that faced him on the desk. He rubbed the back of his neck. *They'll still be here tomorrow*, he decided. "I'd love to, Sterling."

"Great, I've got a tee time at eleven-thirty. See you then."

"Thanks," Will said, as he hung up.

He thought back to what he knew about Sterling Conrad. Nearly the same age as his grandfather, Conrad had been Warren Martin's chief competitor. Will picked up the phone and dialed his grandmother's number. "Gram, I won't be home for lunch. I've got a golf date with Sterling Conrad."

"That's interesting," she said.

"I'm not sure what he wants to talk about, but a round of golf is probably good therapy. I'm not getting much work done on these accounts."

"You know, Will, Sterling worked with your grandfather many years ago. I've never known exactly why he left the agency. All I know is that your grandfather was very disappointed in him, for some reason."

"I didn't know that, Gram, thanks for filling me in. I'll see you tonight." He hung up the phone gently. *I wonder what Sterling Conrad wants.*

4

WILL BENT AND PLACED THE TITLEIST
ON THE TEE. HE USED THE TIP OF ANOTHER
TEE TO SCRATCH SOME DIRT AND GRASS OUT
OF THE GROOVES IN THE FACE OF HIS DRIVER
and then adjusted his stance next to the ball. He gazed down
the fairway toward the far-off green, readjusted his right
foot, and took a practice swing. He stepped up to the ball,
cocked back the club, and drove the ball in a high, clear arc
down the middle of the fairway.

"Good drive," Sterling Conrad said, leaning on his club.
"I think you out-drove me by thirty yards."

The two men started walking down the fairway, dragging their golf carts behind them. The early winter day was crisp and clean. A hint of pale blue smoke hung among the trees. The ground was hard beneath their feet. "Going to be a fast green," said Sterling. "Better be careful when you putt."

Will smiled at the older man. Sterling was dressed in plaid knickers and high-top stockings above his brown and white golf spikes. He had a Tam o'Shanter perched jauntily on his unruly thatch of hair. "Ah, Enid Cook. The dragon at the gate," he laughed, picking up their earlier conversation.

"It's easy for you to laugh, you don't have to work with her every day."

"Now that I'm retired, I don't have to work with anyone," he replied happily.

"You're lucky! I've never seen more people who are about twenty years behind the times than my grandfather's employees."

"Your grandfather was awfully loyal to his employees," Sterling chuckled. "I think everyone he ever hired is still working there. Not much turnover."

"None," Will exclaimed as the two of them reached Sterling's ball.

"Where's the hundred-thirty-five-yard marker?" Sterling searched the edge of the fairway for the small pine tree that he sought. "Oh, there it is. I think I'll use my seven iron." He pulled the club from his bag and addressed the ball. It landed softly on the green, then rolled nearly across it. "I told you we'd have fast greens," he exclaimed.

"I'll be careful," Will said as they approached his ball. "I appreciate the opportunity you've given me to get away from the office for a while. It seems like I'm having to wade through an awful lot of papers to get a handle on how Grandpa ran the agency."

"My pleasure. Even though your grandfather and I were competitors, I don't want to see you fail. Martin Real Estate has been around for over fifty years."

"Well, the more I dig into how the agency was run, the more amazed I am that Grandpa gave you much competition." Will selected the nine iron and chipped the ball gingerly onto the green.

"Good chip, my boy." Sterling leaned on his golf cart. "Your grandfather was an amazing man. There are many people in this town who bless his name. He had the uncanny ability to see right into the heart of the person he was dealing with. Maybe that was his greatest strength, who knows. Whatever it was, it turned him into a successful and wealthy man. But he did have one failing." The older man shook his head.

Will searched Sterling Conrad's face. "And what was that?"

"He was too kind. Too considerate of other people's feelings."

Will nodded his head slowly. "I guess you knew him well. Gram said you used to work with him."

A cloud crossed Sterling's face. "A long time ago, Will, a long time ago. I remember I put together this real estate deal that would have set us up for life. I brought it to him and he seemed to go along until . . . well, I think he lost his nerve. That kind streak of his got in the way."

"Lost his nerve? I guess I don't understand," said Will.

"Said it didn't *feel* right. So he backed out. I tried to raise the money myself but couldn't pull it together without Warren's help. Hunter Hoggard ended up getting the whole deal."

"Hoggard? Are you talking about the Hoggard condominiums on South State Street?"

Sterling pulled his putter from his bag and bent down to size up the green. "You got it." He stroked the ball toward the cup. It ran three feet past and stopped. "Real fast," he exclaimed, looking surprised and annoyed.

"I can remember driving past there when I was just a little boy. Grandpa used to tell us how they tore down four whole blocks of low-income housing to build those luxury condos. He called the place Hog's Heaven. Apparently it put a lot of people out on the street."

"I'll have to admit that's true. On the other hand, Hoggard made millions and set himself up for life. They say opportunity only knocks once. You remember that, my boy, if you're ever going to make Martin Real Estate grow."

Will stroked his ball into the cup.

"Just like your grandfather. You play your best even when it would be politically smart to let an old duffer like me beat you." Sterling tapped his ball into the cup.

Will smiled. "Why did you leave the agency? If you don't mind my asking."

Sterling motioned toward the bench near the ball washer at the side of the next tee. "Well, sort of ties in with the condominium project. Your grandfather proposed that instead of tearing down the low-income housing we look for a piece of undeveloped land and build condominiums there. The big problem was the cost. We found the piece of land but we'd have had to pay to get utility lines run out to it. Then we'd have had to pave the roads. It cost more, much more than just tearing down the buildings on State Street. Anyway, your grandfather went to see Hal Jenkins at the bank. Hal needed a cosigner on the note to guarantee the money for the project."

Sterling turned from Will and looked down the next fairway as if the memory were still painful. A gust of wind swirled scarlet leaves along the edge of the fairway. "Warren asked me to cosign with him. I agreed and we set up a meeting at the bank the next day."

"What happened then?" Will asked, squinting against the strong afternoon light.

"Hoggard called that night and offered me a . . . a bonus, if I'd keep your grandfather from getting the money. He didn't want any competition in the housing market."

Sterling turned and gazed into Will's eyes, seeking understanding.

"And?"

Sterling's shoulders slumped. "The next day I went to the bank with Warren. Three times he asked me to cosign and three times I found an excuse not to. When we got back to the agency your grandfather called me into his office, looked me in the eye, and asked, 'Why?' I made up some cock-and-bull story, but I knew he could see right through me. The next morning I told your grandfather that I was quitting. With the bonus Hoggard gave me I was able to start my own real estate company." His shoulders slumped again as he sighed. "I don't feel much like playing anymore, Will. Would it be okay if we didn't finish the round?"

"I understand," Will said as he stood up from the bench. "Could I ask you one more question, Sterling?"

He shrugged his shoulders. "Sure."

"In the years you knew my grandfather, did he ever mention a woman named Lillian?"

Sterling scratched his head. "Lillian? Not that I can remember. Of course after the banking incident the only conversations I had with your grandfather were business, strictly business."

They walked slowly back to the parking lot in silence. Sterling folded his golf cart and put it in the trunk of his Cadillac. "Your grandfather was one of a kind, my boy."

5

You're not supposed to use the top of the ladder as a step, Will," Ruth Martin reminded her grandson, as he stood on the top of a stepladder replacing a burned-out lightbulb on the front porch. "I'll be careful, Gram. I'm putting in one of those long-life bulbs." He cradled the burned-out bulb in his left hand as he started down the ladder.

"The two of us here together brings back memories, Will."

When he reached the porch, he collapsed the ladder and handed his grandmother the used bulb before carrying the ladder toward the garage. When he returned, his grand-mother was still there, waiting for him.

"Did you ever feel that your grandfather didn't have time for you?"

"What?"

"Did it bother you that it was often just the two of us? After your grandfather died I started remembering a lot of things from those years you lived with us, and I realized that the two of you didn't spend much time together."

"Gram, I think I may have been the one who didn't have enough time for *him* once I graduated from high school. I've felt a little guilty I wasn't here more often before he died. But I never felt he didn't spend enough time with me when I was a kid. I can still see him sitting in the stands at every one of my baseball games."

"I'm glad. I wondered if you felt left out, felt like you really didn't get to know him."

Will looked searchingly at his grandmother. "It's Lillian, isn't it?"

"What do you mean?" Ruth's cheeks colored slightly.

"This whole thing with Lillian. It's making you doubt Grandpa."

"Will, I'd never doubt your grandfather." She handed the bulb back to Will. "I've just been thinking about our life together."

"Gram, how nervous would you be about letting me read some of the journals?"

"Not nervous at all. There are plenty for both of us." As the two of them entered the house, the smell of his grandmother's remarkable meat loaf made Will's mouth water.

"I'll set the table," he said. Soon Ruth brought plates laden with food from the kitchen, and the two of them sat down to eat.

Looking at his grandmother's portrait, Will could not help but notice how strikingly beautiful she had been as a young woman and how regally she had kept that beauty even at seventy-five years of age.

"I played that round of golf with Sterling Conrad this morning," he said.

"Oh? And what's he doing now that he's retired?"

"Playing golf," Will smiled. "And giving advice."

"I've always felt it was too bad he left the agency just when Warren built that development west of town," Ruth said, taking a bite of mashed potatoes.

"What development?" Will asked, putting down his fork and staring at his grandmother.

"Oh, time flies by so fast, I'd forgotten how long ago that was. I guess he'd sold it all to John Squires by the time you were born. It's where the mall is now. We had to mortgage the house and the agency to scrape together the funding, but it proved to be well worth it." She smiled fondly at Will.

"I had no idea."

"As I said, it was a long time ago . . . a long time."

The dinner table was cleared and Will stood beside his grandmother in the kitchen, wiping the dishes as she washed them. "It just seemed like too few dishes to use the dishwasher," she said, happily. "This really is like old times."

After the dishes were put away, Will carried the stack of journals up the stairs to his room, the same room he'd occupied from the time he was a small child. He set the book on the corner of his desk and looked around the room. *It is like old times,* he thought. His baseball trophies rested on top of the bookshelves. He looked at the framed photograph of himself above his old desk. He was nine years old and had just been awarded the most-valuable-player trophy by his Little League coach. His grandfather stood in the background, slightly out of focus, with a proud smile on his face.

Will sighed as he sat in the chair at the desk and examined the spines of the journals. Each had a date printed on it in gold. He scanned the dates, then selected 1966. He opened the black, leather-bound volume and his grandfather's elegant handwriting appeared. Arbitrarily the book had opened to a day in October. Will began to read.

October 25. 7:48 P.M. My first grandson was born today. Samuel and Carol have decided to name him William, after his great-grandfather. I remember clearly the feelings in my heart when my dear Ruth went through the valley of the shadow of death to deliver Samuel. Now he is a father. I thought there could be no joy as great as that which I experienced when I held Samuel in my arms. I was wrong. Tonight I held a small, red-faced baby. With his head in my hand his feet barely reached to my elbow. As I gazed at him, his eyes opened and he struggled to focus on my face. I wondered how much he remembered of the God and Father of us all, who had sent him here so recently. He has tiny fingernails, perfectly formed. I do not remember inspecting Samuel so closely. I am struck by the fact that immortality is in this child. Through him, Samuel and Carol live as Ruth and I live through Samuel. Truly "man is that he might have joy."

Will slowly closed the volume. A smile flickered on his lips as he gazed fondly at the picture above the desk. Then his forehead creased and he searched among the books for 1970. Again the book seemed to fall open to a specific page.

August 12. It is all I can do to write. Today word reached us that Samuel and Carol were involved in an automobile accident. They were driving within the speed limit (although I am not sure what brings me to write that unimportant detail) when a driver heading in the opposite direction apparently fell asleep at the wheel. The car crossed over the center line and hit Samuel and Carol head on. Our sweet Carol died instantly. Samuel survived long enough to reach the hospital, but he was soon pronounced dead.

Not only have we seen our only son die today but we had to make the difficult but important decision to let his organs be donated so others might live. My grief is unbearable. Why couldn't it have been me, rather than Samuel?

Will felt tears welling in his eyes. He thought back to the parents he barely remembered. Finally he forced himself to read further in the diary.

How can we help Will to understand? He is too young to be expected to know the magnitude of his loss. Ruth and I have pledged to raise him as our son. But we know we will never be able to replace his parents. With faith in God we hope the three of us can get over this terrible, terrible loss, but for now our hearts reside in an unfilled pit of mourning gray.

The rest of the page was blank. Will turned to the next page; it, too, was blank. He thumbed through the rest of the journal. All of the rest of the pages were white, unwritten testimony to the loss his grandfather had felt. He gazed at the slightly out-of-focus picture of his grandfather. Tears rolled down his cheeks. He reached out and touched the photograph.

6

WILL SAT AT HIS DESK STARING OUT THE CORNER WINDOW OF THE OFFICE AT THE FALLING SNOW IN THE TOWN SQUARE. HIS DISTRACTED EYES HAD DARK CIRCLES beneath them. Slowly he turned back to the woman who was standing on the other side of his desk.

"Well, Mr. Martin?"

Will focused on Janice Harr, whose graying hair fell to her shoulders. She wore a flowered dress that covered her ample figure. "Well, what?" he asked, blinking his eyes.

"What do you think of their latest offer?" She stared at

Will Martin. Her look made it clear that she did not think he was cut from the same cloth as his grandfather.

"Please, tell me again, what was their offer?"

Janice Harr let out a small, exasperated sigh. "Two hundred thirty thousand dollars."

"Let's hold out for two forty."

"Mr. Martin. We've been negotiating for three weeks. This is their best and final offer. They're set on two thirty, and, quite frankly, it's a fair price."

"John tells me the property is worth at least two forty-five."

Mrs. Harr stared at Will and slowly shook her head. "You're the boss." As she turned to leave, John Henning burst through the door and nearly collided with her. She stiffened noticeably as she brushed past him.

Henning thrust his hand out and grabbed Will's. "Do I detect a lack of enthusiasm in Mrs. Harr?" he observed.

"In her, and in every other agent," replied Will. "I can't believe how resistant to change every one of them is."

"Maybe it's time to shake things up a bit." Henning opened his briefcase and removed a thick binder. "Here's our research findings on Martin Real Estate. It's taken nearly three months of digging to come up with this data."

Will took the proffered report and idly thumbed through it. "It looks pretty complete, John."

"It confirms everything I—we—suspected. This company is living in the nineteen sixties. We need to do some drastic modernization. Quite candidly, most of the agents are way past their prime and we need to introduce some younger people with new ideas and a different way of thinking. Another major discovery is that the rental properties this agency owns haven't had their rents increased in over five years. That's way behind inflation. We need to get those up to market value as soon as possible so we can increase the available cash flow and move ahead with some property acquisitions. And finally, we need to sell off some of the property that is vacant or overvalued, because the taxes alone are killing us."

Will nodded his head absentmindedly. "You're not the first one to make some of these suggestions."

"And this building is so out of date. You need to walk into the other real estate agencies in town and then come back here. It's like opening a door into the past. We need to do some serious remodeling. I've told Miss Cook to contact Wilson Office Supply to get an estimate on all new furniture. It's a first step in making this place look like it's open for business."

"And she agreed?" asked Will.

"Sort of." Henning looked confused and uncertain. "By the way, when's she up for retirement?"

"A generation ago," Will replied, sighing.

John Henning raised an eyebrow. "Well, you've got the report. I hope you read it carefully. I've put a lot of time and effort into it."

"Thanks, John. I will."

He stepped from behind his desk and opened the door for John Henning. As they shook hands, Will noticed Enid Cook staring at them with a definite tightness in her mouth. John Henning looked back at Will and shrugged his shoulders.

The phone rang and Will picked it up. "Martin Real Estate, Will Martin speaking."

"Well, it's good to know you're still alive, Mr. Martin." The playful voice of Julia Welsch flowed over the wire.

"Hello, Julia. I've been meaning to call you."

"That's nice to hear. I'm calling to see if you're available for dinner tonight. I'm not trying to be pushy, but I'd love to see you," she purred.

Will gazed out the window. "I'd really like to, Julia, but I'm pretty busy. John Henning just dropped off this massive report he's done on the agency and I need to go over it tonight." He fingered the corner of the binder on his desk.

"I see." He could hear the coldness in her voice.

"Julia . . . soon. I've just got to get these things taken care of. I don't have much time before I have to return to New York City. I can't expect Cauley, French and Partridge to hold my position open forever."

"I know, I understand." He could hear her voice softening. "I've always liked New York City. I can't wait for us to go skating with the Davidsons."

Will wrinkled his brow. "Sure," he said, "the Davidsons."

"At Rockefeller Center," she reminded him. "I'll be waiting for your call the minute you're free."

"Thanks, Julia. Talk to you soon." As he hung up, Will looked absently out the window. The light snow still fell in the town square as a nighttime breeze sent it swirling into the glow from the curved, iron streetlamps that had rimmed the square since before the First World War. Will put on his overcoat and retrieved the binder from his desk. After weighing it in his hands, he placed it back on the desk.

"Are you leaving, Mr. Martin?" Enid Cook asked.

He nodded his head. "Good night, Miss Cook," he said as he walked by.

"Mr. Martin," she whispered in a conspiratorial tone. Will stopped and turned around. "I still don't like Mr. Henning."

"Good night, Miss Cook," he said more firmly, and closed the door behind him. The snow-capped peaks to the east could be seen against the pale blue-black of the early night sky. The wind blew briskly in his face as he walked toward his car.

Will drove slowly home and felt oddly relieved when the front porch light greeted him.

"You look tired, Will. Is anything wrong?" Ruth Martin asked as they lingered around the dinner table.

"Just lots of pressure, Gram. I think Grandpa kept some of the people at the agency too long."

"Oh? Like who?"

"Enid Cook, for one," he said.

"Will, move slowly. A wise man listens more than he speaks and observes more than he sees."

"Thank you, Gram. I hope I'll make decisions that will please you." He covered a great yawn and smiled. "I think I'll turn in early tonight."

"I think I will, too, Will."

After they cleared the table, he squeezed her hand and slowly climbed the stairs to his bedroom. Absently he picked up one of the journals from his desk, then thought better of it and prepared for bed. The house began to settle down for the night. The familiar sound of the furnace hum-chunked in the background. Will lay in the dark, eyes wide open, staring at the ceiling. His mind raced with thoughts of the agency, Julia, Lillian, and his grandfather. Then something out of sync registered in his brain. He blinked his eyes and strained his ears. The sound came again. Slowly Will climbed out of bed, threw a robe around his shoulders, and opened his door. He was walking quietly down the hallway to his grandmother's room when he heard the sound again. It was coming from downstairs.

Quickly he moved down the stairs, ears and eyes alert. He heard the sound again, from his grandfather's office. Will turned the knob slowly and the door opened noiselessly. He felt a rush of cold air on his bare feet, as he flipped on the light switch. A window was open a few inches and the breeze was causing the crystal pendants hanging from the Tiffany lamp on the top of the desk to tinkle. He walked to the window and closed it. The pages of a journal had blown open. Will looked at the page.

December 24. Ruth and Will have gone shopping. It is time to visit Lillian.

Will felt as if a cold fist had hit him in the stomach. Quickly he grabbed a half-dozen volumes from the shelf and retreated to the kitchen. He opened the next journal to December 24.

Time to visit Lillian.

Each of the other journals had the same entry on Christmas Eve. Will sat dejectedly at the table and opened the last volume. This time the entry was larger.

December 24. Another year has passed. There is pain in my heart that I deceive Ruth by not telling her about my visits to Lillian. But I am sure it would cause her even more pain, and I'd rather avoid that.

Will closed the book and looked blankly at the wall. "Grandpa," he whispered, "how could you?" He returned the books to the office and climbed the stairs to spend another restless night in bed.

7

ON MONDAY MORNING WILL AWOKE LATE, AMAZED THAT HE HAD SLEPT AT ALL. HE QUICKLY SHOWERED, SHAVED, AND DRESSED FOR THE OFFICE. AS HE RACED down the stairs, he savored the smell of frying bacon. He hurried into the kitchen and pulled the refrigerator door open. He retrieved a tumbler from the cupboard and poured it full of orange juice, downing it in a single gulp, before grabbing a slice of toast from the waiting stack on the table. He heard the front door open and close.

"Sleep well?" his grandmother asked, walking into the room with the morning paper.

He shook his head. "Passably well. Good morning, Gram." He finished stuffing the slice of toast into his mouth and poured himself a cup of coffee. "By the way, had you been reading Grandpa's journals in the office last evening before you went to bed?"

Ruth thought for a moment. "Yes, I guess I was. Why?"

"Oh, nothing. The window was open in there when I went down to check on a noise I heard."

"I opened it, Will. It gets warm in there with the fireplace. I guess I forgot to close it." She took off her apron. "You look tired, dear."

"I'm not sleeping well lately, but I'm young. I'll survive." He kissed his grandmother's cheek and turned to go.

"Come now, you need more than a piece of toast for breakfast. What am I going to do with all of this food?"

"Invite someone over. You used to have the neighbor ladies over all the time." He waved good-bye and disappeared down the hall. A moment later she heard the front door open and close.

Ruth sighed and started to clear the food from the table, but as she did she thought about what Will had said. She put down the food and walked slowly to the phone. She dialed a number from memory. The phone rang. "Hello," said a feeble voice on the other end.

"Hello, Margaret. This is Ruth Martin. Do you have time for breakfast? I haven't heard about how your grand-children are doing for the longest time."

"Ruth, it's good to hear your voice. When do you want to eat?"

"Right now, Margaret, it's on the table. Why don't you just hurry next door, I'll be waiting."

"I'll be over as fast as these old legs can move me," she answered excitedly. "Good-bye."

A few moments later the back door bell rang, and Ruth went to greet her next-door neighbor. "Margaret, it's so good to have you here again. Have a seat."

Margaret Sweet slowly lowered her bulky frame into a chair at the kitchen table. "Ruth, you always were the best cook," she gushed as she spread a piece of toast with grape jelly. "Bacon and eggs, my favorite." She scooped a healthy serving of scrambled eggs onto her plate and crumbled crisp bacon over the top of the eggs. She held another strip of bacon up to her mouth and began to nibble on it. "How do you make it so crispy, Ruth?"

Ruth smiled at her neighbor. Will was right; it was time she started renewing her acquaintances. "You just have to put the bacon into a cold pan and let it warm up slowly until it's crisp, Margaret. It just takes a little time."

"You always were more patient than I," Margaret smiled. The two women chatted as they ate. Finally, Margaret looked at Ruth over the top of her eyeglasses and said, "How are you doing?"

"Fine, fine. I have no reason to complain."

"Really, how are you doing? You and Warren were so close it must be a terrible shock to be without him. I mean, at least when my Collin died he'd been sick for so long it was almost a blessing. But Warren. So quickly." Margaret shook her head as if she found it hard to believe what had happened.

"I'm fine, dear, really. Warren was so independent that I sometimes think it's better he went when he was still active. He could never have faced having others take care of him." She smiled a faint smile. "I'm fine."

Margaret spread jelly onto another slice of toast and bit into it. "I don't want to pry, but did he leave you enough to live on?"

"Oh, yes. I'm quite comfortable. Warren made some very prudent investments and I have more, much more than I need."

"Well, he was so thoughtful, so giving. I'm glad my Collin listened to him when Warren gave him advice on purchasing those four hundred acres out in the foothills. Once he got the well drilled we were able to plant the whole thing in grapevines. As long as the world keeps drinking grape juice I have no worries."

"More to eat?" Ruth asked her neighbor.

"No, thank you, I've had more than enough, but you did ask about my grandchildren." She pulled a small album from the pocket of her dress. The two women looked at the pictures of grandchildren for several minutes. Finally, Margaret replaced the album in her pocket. "Thank you for inviting me over. It's been a long time since we got together. We need to do it more often."

The two women walked through the dining room and Margaret gazed fondly at the painting of Warren Martin. "What a dear, kind man he was," she said. "I often envied the two of you, you were so close. I'm sure there was never a moment in your marriage that you doubted each other's love."

Ruth's eyes clouded with unbidden tears. *Oh Warren,* she thought.

"I'll let myself out," Margaret said, patting her arm.

8

WILL POINTED TO THE STREET FROM THE TOP-STORY WINDOW OF THE VACANT BUILDING. "MR. SPELLMAN, LOOK AT THIS VIEW OF THE TOWN SQUARE THAT YOU HAVE not only from this office, but from every office on the front of the building."

Ray Spellman nodded his head. "Spectacular. Especially with this pretty layer of snow covering everything."

Will smiled and the two men walked slowly down the stairway. Spellman thumped his hand against the wall.

"Lathe and plaster, not wallboard," he said. "They don't build them like this anymore."

Will nodded in agreement. "It's a grand old building, Mr. Spellman."

The two of them walked out the front door and looked up at the deep red sandstone facade of the building. A rising sun had been carved into the stone above the door. Each window arch was capped with an intricately carved keystone. "Quite a building, Will. You really caught me by surprise when you called. I didn't think you'd ever sell it. Did you know it was the first building your grandfather ever bought after he opened Martin Real Estate?"

"So I've heard. But it hasn't had a tenant for nearly a year."

"Well, that should tell you something," Spellman said logically. "Just keep it in mind when you determine how much you're going to try to get out of me."

Will turned his hands palm up and shrugged his shoulders. "It may have been mismanaged, but you know what they say about real estate, Ray. Location, location..."

"I know, I know." Spellman said stamping his feet to keep them warm.

Will turned and faced the building again. "And as you saw, this building has the premier view of the square." He turned to look at the pretty, bustling scene going on around him.

Spellman looked up and down the front of the building with a practiced eye. "Will, if you were your grandfather I'd say let's shake hands on it and we'll work out the details later, but I suspect you'll want something more substantial. Call me when you're ready to discuss the price."

The two men shook hands and Spellman slid into the seat of his Lincoln Continental. The electric window slid down as he started the car. "Let me know if anyone else shows interest, okay?"

"You can count on it," Will said, nodding his head. Spellman waved good-bye as the car pulled away from the curb. Will smiled and walked quickly across the square toward his office. The crust of the snow crackled under his feet.

Enid Cook's jaw was rigid as Will passed her desk on the way to his office. He felt her eyes bore into him as he closed the door. He hung his coat on the coat rack and sat down in the swivel chair. He gazed out the window toward the sandstone building across the square and began trying to imagine his grandfather as a young man buying his first piece of real estate. The phone rang. "Martin Real Estate, this is Will," he said.

"Hello, Will, I'm really not trying to put you on the spot, but I wonder what you're doing for lunch." It was Julia.

Will flipped opened his day book. "Nothing on my calendar," he replied pleasantly. "Where would you like to go?"

"How about Pallermo's? It's close by and they have great food."

"I'll meet you there in ten minutes. Okay?" Will glanced at his watch.

"I thought you'd never ask," Julia laughed.

Will hung up the phone and walked back into the main office. "I'll be back in an hour or so," he said to Enid Cook, as he pulled on his topcoat.

"Yes, Mr. Martin," she replied icily. "Do you think you'll have time to go over the end-of-year report any time soon?" But Will had already closed the door.

He climbed into his Jaguar and ten minutes later he was pulling into Pallermo's parking lot. Julia waved at him from her window seat. He entered the restaurant and inhaled the heady aroma of garlic and cheese. Julia rose from her seat and gave him a warm kiss. As they sat down, she reached over and covered his hand with hers.

"It has been a while. Still busy at the office?"

Will nodded his head.

"And what about Lillian? Any leads?"

"Not yet."

The waiter appeared and offered them menus. "I know what I want," she said smiling. "The shrimp pasta salad and a Diet Coke." She looked expectantly at Will.

"I'll have the chicken parmesan with a side salad, house dressing. Water will be fine."

The waiter gave a slight bow and left.

"You do look tired, Will."

He smiled. "Everyone tells me that. I guess I've been putting in some pretty long hours and reading my grandfather's journals at night. They give me so much to think about that I find it hard to sleep."

"Are you finding any more hints to the mystery woman?"

"A line or two here and there. But in one of his entries Grandpa admitted that he felt guilty about deceiving Gram."

"I hate to say it, but I told you so."

"I know you did."

Julia patted his hand. "Look, I'm not justifying his behavior, but he's far from alone, you know. Many, many happily married men have a fling."

Will pulled his hand away. "Just because everybody's doing it, doesn't make it okay."

Julia waved her hand back and forth. "I'm not saying that at all. It's just that these things can happen."

Will leaned toward her. "They aren't supposed to. Not in my family."

Julia reached out and took his hand. "You're so uptight, Will."

"Not uptight as much as disappointed."

"And angry. I can tell you're angry." Julia traced her finger on the back of Will's hand. "Probably with good cause. After all, it's hard to see someone you've always thought of as the perfect man fall in your estimation. I can understand why you're angry."

Will shrugged his shoulders. "Maybe a little."

Julia leaned forward conspiratorially. "Will, give it up. There's just no reason to have you—and your grand-mother—so upset. I know you think all the answers are in those books, but what if they aren't? What's the next step? Taking out an advertisement in the local papers? This search for Lillian could become terribly embarrassing."

Will withdrew his hand again. "It certainly is difficult to talk about, that's for sure."

"Well, then just drop it!" Julia straightened in her chair.

At that moment the waiter reappeared with their food and placed it carefully on the table. Will welcomed the break in the conversation.

"We should talk about something else while we eat," he suggested as the waiter turned away.

"Absolutely," Julia said brightening. "Do you want me to confirm the reservations for our New York trip? Or will you?"

"Julia, I'll confirm the reservations and pay for your hotel room, but I'm not going to be able to go," he replied. "I'm really sorry."

"What . . . why?"

"A number of reasons, the most important being that I'm just not comfortable turning the office over to John

Henning, yet. There's so much that still has to be decided, and my time here, as I've explained, is short. I just can't get away. I should have realized this was a bad time for me to try to get away."

"Will, we've been planning this for weeks," Julia said, her eyes glacial beneath hooded lids and her mouth a thin line. "I've committed to the Davidsons."

"I'm sorry. Perhaps you can invite a friend to go with you and I'll pay both of your expenses. It's the least I can do," Will said, looking miserable.

Julia fixed him with a withering gaze. "The next thing I know you'll be canceling our date to the Christmas Ball at the Country Club."

"No, no," Will protested. "I'll be there, I promise." He shifted his gaze to his plate. "When is it, again?"

"You have *got* to be kidding," she spat out.

"Well," said Will lamely, "Saturday night, right?"

"Friday."

"Friday, of course. I'll write it down." Will quickly signaled the waiter as Julia's beautiful blue eyes burned into his face.

"I'll get this," Will said, surveying their uneaten food before grabbing the check and hurrying to the cash register.

9

There was a definite chill in the air as Will parked the Jaguar in the garage. *Could be more snow on the way,* he thought, rubbing his hands together as he entered the front hall. The reassuring scent of wood smoke had greeted him as he opened the front door. "Gram," he called out as he hung up his coat. "I'm home."

"I'm in the office, dear."

He found his grandmother sitting at the table in the office wrapping Christmas gifts. Rolls of paper lay in disarray around her. "I have to get these in the mail, if they're going to get to Walter and Edith," she said.

"Can I help?" Will asked, pulling a chair to the table.

"An extra pair of hands is always appreciated, dear. How was your day?" Ruth asked, taking the adhesive strip off of a big red bow and pressing it on a snowflake-covered box.

Will made a roller-coaster movement with his hand. "Some ups, some downs . . . you know," he replied. After a moment of thought he continued, "Gram, can I ask you a question?"

"Of course, dear."

"You've met Julia. What's your impression?"

"She's an extremely pretty young woman, Will," his grandmother said with a smile.

"Uh huh." Will began tying ribbon around the gift he was wrapping. "Gram, I dated quite a few women in New York. Julia reminds me of them, chic and sophisticated and image-conscious."

"Do you miss the big city?" Ruth picked up another package and selected a sheet of wrapping paper.

"Sometimes, but the longer I'm here, the less anxious I am to get back. Still, there are two things I miss . . . the excitement and the anonymity."

"Anonymity?" she raised an eyebrow. "In that huge city?"

"That's just it, Gram. It's so big that you have privacy. You can be famous and nobody at the same time."

"I'm not sure I understand, Will."

"Being home, back here with you, I'd forgotten how everybody knows everything about everybody else."

"Do you think that's a bad thing?"

Will chewed on his lower lip for a moment. "It depends. In New York no one knows anything unless it makes the morning paper. Here people know if you don't pick up the morning paper from your lawn."

Ruth looked at her grandson. "How soon until you and Julia leave for New York?"

Will concentrated on the gift he was wrapping. "I'm not going to the city with her, Gram. I canceled."

"Oh, really," his grandmother exhaled slowly.

Will reached for a name tag. "But maybe now would be a good time for *you* to get away. I could take care of the house while you took a Christmas cruise. Hawaii maybe? A Christmas gift from me to you."

Ruth glanced sideways at Will. "Meaning you haven't been able to find out anything more about Lillian?"

"Saw right through me, didn't you?"

"Will, a cruise isn't what I want for Christmas. But I'll understand if you aren't able to deliver my request."

The two of them continued wrapping presents in silence as the fire crackled and popped merrily in the fireplace. Will finished filling out the tag on a present, cleared his throat, and asked the question that had been worrying him since

Thanksgiving. "Gram, are you sure, really sure, you want to know who Lillian is? Maybe it would be better for everyone concerned if we just forgot about her."

Ruth folded her hands and placed them in her lap. "I'd like that, Will. I really would. But I can't forget . . . that's the problem."

Will looked at the grandmother who had raised him and slowly nodded his head. "I understand." She turned to look at him. "Gram, this is really hard, but did you and Grandpa fight? I can't ever remember hearing an unkind word spoken in our house, but, when you're a kid, sometimes you miss things."

Ruth stared into the fire. "Oh, we had our ups and downs. Every couple does. You think you know someone extremely well and then you get married and find out you've married a stranger. You grow up thinking everyone in the world does things the same way your family does them and then you find out the man you married grew up in a whole different world. And if you live together for more than half a century, you're bound to disagree at times."

Will waited patiently while his grandmother seemed lost in thought.

"There was one time, though, that was the lowest point in our marriage. When your father and mother died, Will, it took me a lot longer to get over it than it took Warren. I think he rebounded quite quickly. I was angry with him . . . thought he wasn't grieving enough. I thought he buried himself in his business. It took me over a year to stop thinking during every waking hour about the accident that took your parents. It was a hard time for both of us. We each withdrew into our own cocoon. I blame myself more than I blame your grandfather."

"I don't know if you've read the journal for that year," Will said softly, "but the last entry was the night my parents died. And there wasn't a journal for the next year, either."

Ruth nodded her head. "I discovered that, too."

Will fiddled with the wrapping paper he was taping around a small box. "January of nineteen seventy-two he started writing again. My guess is he made a New Year's resolution to begin keeping his journal again. The first mention of Lillian comes in December of that year, so he must have met her between nineteen seventy and seventy-two. During that time when you were struggling hardest. He never gives any details. It's just a date and a time for their meeting."

"I think it may have been someone at the agency," Ruth said quietly. "That's where Warren found solace from his grief."

"You mean someone who worked there?" asked Will.

"Or someone they sold a house to." Suddenly Gram's voice took on an excited quality. "Will, Enid Cook has worked at the agency since the very beginning. If anyone would know, she would." She saw Will shake his head. "What's the matter?"

"Here we are discussing someone Grandpa may have had an affair with just as if we were discussing the weather. It seems kind of weird."

"Are you uncomfortable talking to me about Lillian?"

"Well, yes. I mean, you're my grandmother." He shifted uncomfortably in his seat.

"If I've learned anything, Will, it's this. It's better to talk about things and get them out in the open than to keep them hidden and festering. There are abscesses of the soul just as surely as there are abscesses of the body."

Ruth stood and walked to the fireplace. She rested her hand on the mantel. Will stared at this regal woman for a moment. "You're right, Gram. I'll just have to redouble my efforts. I'm serious about getting you your gift before Christmas Eve. But as for getting help from Enid Cook, the only help she'd give me is a swift kick out the door."

"Oh? Your grandfather thought quite highly of her, I believe."

"Gram, we're from two different planets."

Ruth fingered the pine boughs that decorated the mantel. She crushed some needles and smelled her fingers. "Then what about Renee?"

"Who?" Will asked.

"Renee Carr. I'm sure you've met her. She was your grandfather's secretary for a few years."

Will looked thoughtful. "Renee? Was she the redhead?"

"That's the one. She was a darling girl, sharp as a tack. She knew everything that went on in the office. Your grandfather was sorry when she left. But she got married and began operating a dance studio down on Bellfontaine. I heard that she's divorced now. I wonder if she could help."

Will glanced at his watch. "I'll try to get hold of her in the morning."

"I don't think I'd mention it to Julia," Gram smiled pleasantly and returned to her gift wrapping.

10

A STRONG WIND DEVELOPED DURING THE NIGHT AND A FEW FLAKES OF SNOW WERE BEING DRIVEN ALMOST SIDEWAYS AS WILL ENTERED HIS OFFICE. ENID COOK WAS already sitting at her desk. She glanced up at Will and then continued to type. He went into his office, took off his coat, and shut the door. He sat in the swivel chair and looked out the window at the town square. The wind had blown most of the snow from the trees and their limbs stood like dark fingers pointing at the skies. They waved back and forth with the strong gusts. He could clearly see

the sandstone face of his grandfather's first building across the square. The dark windows stared back at him. A light came on in Mick's Flower Shop. Slowly he got to his feet and walked to the door.

"Miss Cook?"

"Yes, Mr. Martin?"

"Do you happen to know where Renee Carr's dance studio is?"

Enid's left eyebrow moved up noticeably. "Yes, Mr. Martin, I do."

Will waited patiently.

"Do you know where Anderson's shoe store is located?" Will nodded his head. "The dance studio is above the shoe store."

"Thank you, Miss Cook. I don't suppose you know her telephone number?"

"No, Mr. Martin, I don't," Enid said coolly, turning back to her typewriter.

I wonder how long it would take her to learn how to use a word processor. Somehow the thought made him smile. He returned to his desk and started going through a stack of papers near the phone. A jumble of thoughts competed for attention. He tried immersing himself in the contracts that lay before him, but his mind kept shifting to the unknown Lillian. He tried to force himself to think about the work at hand, but the morning hours crept by slowly. Finally at twelve o'clock he gave up.

"Miss Cook," he said, as he walked from his office. "I'm gone for the rest of the day if anyone asks."

"Oh, really, Mr. Martin? I was under the impression this office remained open until six o'clock."

Will felt his cheeks growing warm. "I'm sure you and the other agents can take good care of things here," he called over his shoulder, as he escaped into the coolness of the winter afternoon. He drove quickly to Anderson's shoe store. He had never noticed the second door leading from the parking lot. Carefully stenciled on the door were the words CARR DANCE STUDIO and beneath it, ONE FLIGHT UP. He opened the door and climbed the steep stairway. He could hear the squeal of excited voices as he reached the top of the stairs.

The entire second floor of the building had been turned into a dance studio. Mirrors lined the wall opposite the windows. A practice bar ran the length of the mirrored wall. The floor had been painted a flat black and the half dozen miniature ballerinas in pink and white tutus stood out as if illuminated by a spotlight.

Renee Carr was dressed in black leotards that accentuated her slim figure. She ran her hand through the tight curls of her reddish brown hair. "Monica, please hold onto the bar."

A small set of bleachers was placed adjacent to the stairway. A small boy, attentive to what was happening in the room, sat on the bottom row with a boom box next to him. Renee nodded to him and he punched a button on the cassette player. The notes of Tchaikovsky's "Nutcracker Suite" filled the studio. "Hi," Will said, sitting down next to the boy.

The child shifted his gaze from the dancers to Will. "I'm the music man," he said, while pointing his thumb at his chest and nodding his head up and down.

"Hi, music man, I'm Will Martin." He extended his hand and they shook.

The boy focused on the dancers again. "Not many dads come here. Mostly moms. That's my mom out there teaching the class."

"That so?" Will said. "Well, I'm not a dad, but I am here to see your mom."

At that moment Renee Carr looked across the studio at her son and the nice-looking man sitting on the bleachers. "Shhh," she said, placing her finger in front of her lips.

"That's Mom," the boy whispered. Soon his mother looked at him and drew the edge of her hand across her throat. "That means stop the music." He punched another button.

The little girls gathered around Renee. "It's coming along, it's coming along," she said. "But you girls are going to have to settle down and practice more. The Christmas program's three weeks away. You need to have your costumes ready a week before so we can have them for dress rehearsal." The girls milled around like a small flock of birds.

Will heard the outside door open, followed by the sound of feet on the stairs. The mothers of the dancers soon appeared and joined the general excitement. Before long, the women wrapped their charges in coats to ward off the winter chill and hustled them down the stairs. Renee watched them go. She slowly shook her head with a smile on her face.

"Mom, come meet somebody."

Renee Carr walked over to the bleachers and extended her hand.

"You're Will Martin. We've met before."

Will shook her hand. "You have a good memory."

"Your grandfather—Warren—wouldn't let me forget. He talked about you constantly." She began ticking items off on her fingertips. "As I recall you were going to be a professional baseball player—first base—then you were hoping to be the next Perry Mason, but you opted out for Harvard Business School instead, and then—"

"Stop, please," Will smiled. "Pretty impressive. I hope he left out *some* of the details."

"Maybe, but darn few, I'll bet. What can I do for you? Dance lessons?" She laughed a deep, throaty laugh.

"Actually it's a little complicated. It has to do with a Christmas gift for my grandmother." The boy pulled the cord from the wall socket and began putting the cassette player away. "I was hoping that maybe you could help. Do you have a few minutes?"

The boy lugged the black plastic box to a closet in the corner. "I'm sorry, but I don't have any time right now. I really need to get Justin home."

"Justin? Oh, the music man," Will said, smiling.

"I have to eat lunch, and get to the skating rink for class," Justin said, as he closed the closet.

Will turned back to Renee. "Could I have fifteen minutes tomorrow?"

"Classes all day," said Renee, a little too quickly.

"Oh," Will said softly. "I see."

Justin reached up and took his mother's hand.

"Perhaps another time, then? It was nice seeing you again and nice meeting you, Justin." Will shook the boy's hand.

"Mom, he could come over for dinner." The boy blurted out the words and then smiled as though enjoying their confused silence.

"Honey, Mr. Martin is very busy," she replied uncomfortably.

Justin looked into Will's face. "You have to eat dinner, don't you?"

Renee's face turned scarlet. *"Justin,"* she said, through partly clenched teeth.

Will looked at the boy and then Renee. "Actually, Justin, you're right, I do have to eat dinner. The real question is, does your mother want to eat tomorrow night?"

"Yup," Justin said quickly, "we eat every night."

Renee closed her eyes and took a deep breath. "The candor of a six-year-old." She lowered her eyes to the floor, then said quietly, "We *will* be eating dinner tomorrow night, if you'd like to come, Mr. Martin."

"Thank you, Mrs. Carr. I accept your, er, Justin's invitation."

"Neat!" said Justin. "What time, Mom?"

"Seven o'clock," she replied, looking suddenly amused and giving a small shake of her head.

Will looked at her and raised his eyebrows. "Seven o'clock then. I'll bring dessert."

"Great. Thanks. Our address is 972 Church Road." Renee flipped a switch and the lights in the studio went out. She led Will and Justin down the stairway toward the dim light at the bottom of the steps. "Maybe I can help you, Will," she said as she opened the door to the parking lot.

"Help me?" He felt suddenly confused.

"With a Christmas gift for your grandmother. Your grandfather's favorite store for Christmas gifts was Taylor's."

"Taylor's?" Will wrinkled his forehead. "Oh, the jewelry store."

"That's right," she replied. "He loved getting your grandmother gifts from there."

"Thank you . . . Renee," Will ventured.

"We'll see you tomorrow night," she called over her shoulder.

A light snow was falling as Will waited for Renee and Justin to drive off in their old Chevrolet. He opened the door of the Jaguar and glanced at his watch. *Taylor's,* he thought, as he closed the door and pulled out of the parking lot.

11

WILL MADE HIS WAY THROUGH THE THRONG OF SHOPPERS IN THE MIDDLE OF TOWN. HE GLANCED AT HIS WATCH AGAIN; IT WAS JUST PAST ONE. THE ORNATE GOLD-leaf sign hanging above the display window at Taylor's beckoned to him. "Excuse me," he said, as he brushed against a woman walking with a large package. Will slowly pushed open the heavy door of Taylor's Jewelry and entered the plush elegance of the shop. A small silver bell above the doorway tinkled as he closed the door.

The walls were lined with glass cases filled with glittering jewelry. A horseshoe-shaped counter extended from the back wall into the room. Behind the counter a middle-aged woman was showing an assortment of wristwatches to a customer who had removed his camel-hair coat and folded it on the chair beside him.

"I'll be with you shortly," she said in a melodious voice, smiling at Will.

He nodded in her direction and bent closer to the countertop nearest him. He was admiring an assortment of ruby rings when an older man appeared from a back room. He was tall and thin and wore a dark blue pin-striped suit. A gold chain spanned his vest. "Yes, sir, may I help you?"

Will smiled and extended his hand. "Mr. Taylor?"

"Yes," the older man replied, shaking his hand.

"My name is Will Martin. Warren Martin was my grandfather."

"Oh, how nice to meet you," Mr. Taylor beamed. "Your grandfather was one of the finest men I've ever been blessed to meet."

"I'm glad you thought so highly of him."

"I'm not just saying it," Mr. Taylor insisted. "Warren Martin was the most Christ-like man I ever knew."

"I'm discovering that many people feel as you do," Will replied, feeling proud and suddenly humble at the same time.

"I'm sure they do. What can I do for you, son?"

"I've been told that my grandfather often bought gifts for my grandmother here. Is that true?"

A warm smile spread over Taylor's face. "Yes, yes. That is correct, my boy, he told me he wouldn't trust anyone else when it came to buying jewelry for Mrs. Martin. He remained loyal even when the town grew and my competition increased. Loyalty was one of his greater attributes. Of course, he was responsible for much of this town's growth."

Will nodded his head in agreement.

"Will!" Someone called from the front of the store. He turned to see Julia standing there, smiling. "I thought that was you. I was just walking by on my way to lunch when I looked in the window and..."

"Ah, Miss Welsch," said Mr. Taylor, with a slight bow.

"Hello, Mr. Taylor." She walked over and shook his hand.

"Hi, Julia," Will said, admiring the way her blue wool hat accentuated her face and made her eyes an even deeper blue.

"What brings you here?" she asked.

"I'm doing some Christmas shopping," he replied.

Julia suddenly spotted the display of rings between Will and Mr. Taylor, and a smile formed on her lips. "Oh," she gasped. "I'm sorry. I'd better be on my way." She gave Will a quick kiss on the cheek, whirled around, and hurried to the door. Just before she left the store, she looked back at Will, and smiled broadly and winked.

Taylor watched her leave. "I didn't know you and Miss Welsch..."

"We've dated a little," said Will uncomfortably. "But if the truth be known I really came in to see about a gift for my grandmother."

Mr. Taylor's eyebrows rose and he suddenly snapped his fingers. "But of course. I really should have contacted you before now. A moment, please." He quickly disappeared through the door into the back room.

Soon Mr. Taylor reappeared holding a large velvet box. "At your grandfather's request I created this piece for your grandmother. Unfortunately, he passed away before it was completed. But this is perfect. You can deliver to her a very special Christmas present."

Will took the box and opened it. Inside was an exquisite emerald pendant hanging on a liquid gold chain. He removed it and looked deep into the stone. "It's beautiful, breathtaking, Mr. Taylor," he said reverently. "I don't believe I've ever seen anything quite like this."

The jeweler nodded his head. "Your grandfather had a good eye for quality, Mr. Martin. He had me acquire several emeralds before he picked this one. He wanted this birthstone necklace to be perfect."

"Birthstone? An emerald? I guess I never realized an emerald was a birthstone. I'm sure my grandmother will be more than pleased." He smiled at the thought of his grandfather choosing this particular stone for Gram.

"Yes, yes," Taylor replied. "I've always envied women with May birthdays."

Will felt as if a sword had pierced his soul.

"Does it pass your inspection, Mr. Martin?" Taylor replaced the pendant in the velvet box.

"It's beautiful," Will said with a forced smile. "What do I owe you, Mr. Taylor?"

"Nothing, nothing at all, Mr. Martin. Your grandfather paid for this gift at the time he picked out the stone." He placed the velvet box in a small bag. "We're just glad to be of service. I hope you'll use us in the future." He patted Will on the shoulder as he handed him the present.

The cold air slapped Will in the face as he left the jewelry store. He looked at the bag he was carrying. *An emerald for a May birthday. Gram was born in September.*

12

WILL MARCHED INTO HIS OFFICE, SHUT
THE DOOR, AND DROPPED HEAVILY INTO THE
SWIVEL CHAIR. HE DANGLED THE BAG FROM
TAYLOR'S FROM HIS INDEX FINGER. *SHE HAD
to be someone Grandpa knew well,* he thought. *Why only on
Christmas Eve? I haven't seen any other mention . . .* Suddenly he sat
upright.

Enid Cook opened the door to his office. "Mr. Martin,
I didn't expect you back, but as long as you're here can we
look at the end-of-the-year report?"

"I'm sorry to keep putting you off, Miss Cook. Perhaps later today. Right now I need to look at some of the records from past years."

Enid blinked her eyes. "What kinds of records?"

"I need to see the W-4 forms and the list of clients we served."

"For which years, Mr. Martin?"

"To begin with, let me see the records for nineteen seventy through seventy-two."

"They're not here. They're in storage."

"And where is that, Miss Cook?"

Enid's face blanched. "Why do you want to know, Mr. Martin?"

Will ignored the look on Enid's face. "Just tell me where they are, Miss Cook. I need to see those files."

"I'll get you the keys," she said, as she backed out of the office.

Will followed her to her desk. She fished a set of keys from the bottom drawer and handed it to him. "This key opens the front door at Redwood Storage. The number of our storage room is on the other key."

"Thank you, Miss Cook. I'll be at Redwood Storage if anyone needs me." He left the office and walked swiftly to his car.

A skiff of snow covered the streets as Will made his way across town to the storage facility. He glanced at Julia's condominium complex as he passed by. Redwood Storage was in an area of town that Will rarely frequented, but he finally located it among a group of run-down buildings. The key Enid Cook had given him opened the front door to reveal a hallway lined on both sides with numbered doors. He glanced at the key. Number 714. There was no elevator, so Will slowly climbed the stairs to the seventh floor. A light switch on each landing turned on a row of dim lights hanging from the ceiling. He made his way down the hallway until he found number 714. The key opened the door to reveal a room about twelve by fifteen feet lined with storage boxes. There was a small window at one end, but it let in little light. He flipped on a light switch near the door and began examining the labels. Three boxes stacked near the back of the small chamber were marked 1970. Will pulled the top box off the stack and blew away the dust. He used a small pocketknife to slit the tape that held the box closed. Inside were file folders labeled January through May.

He took off his jacket and sat on the floor next to the box. "Lillian, where are you?" he asked, removing the first folder and sifting through the papers. Will scanned each document quickly. There was no mention of Lillian. Two hours later he had completed all of the boxes from 1970. He started on 1971. As he was finishing the first box from that year he discovered that his legs had gone to sleep. He stretched them out slowly and then staggered to his feet and stood grimacing as feeling returned to his legs. He retrieved the second box and knelt on the floor while he made his way through the file folders. By the time he finished inspecting all of the boxes up to 1972, the sun had set and a stiff wind blew swirls of snow around the building. Will carefully restacked the boxes and locked the door behind him.

The Jaguar stood with small drifts of snow blown against its tires. Will pushed the button on his key ring and unlocked the doors. He slid into the driver's seat and started the car. Except for the wind, there was no other sound but the purring of the engine. He sat there for several minutes waiting for the car to warm up. The windshield wipers created arched windows through the snow. Will sat in silent contemplation, then shifted into gear and drove home.

He pulled the car into the garage and walked into the kitchen. His grandmother stood at the sink wiping a plate. Will kissed her on the cheek and went over to the sink to wash his hands.

"Ready for dinner, dear? You look exhausted."

He shook his head. "I've been over at Redwood Storage going through all of the records from nineteen seventy through seventy-two. I checked every employee. I went through every business transaction that occurred." He walked across the kitchen. "I found a lot of interesting names, but no Lillian." He waved his hand idly, then dropped it to his side. "I'm sorry, Gram. I'm not very hungry."

Ruth watched her grandson climb the stairs to his bedroom. "What have I done?" she whispered. "Warren, what have you done?"

13

WILL ARRIVED AT THE AGENCY EARLY THE NEXT MORNING. HE HAD SPENT ANOTHER RESTLESS NIGHT AND DID NOT FEEL UP TO A CONFRONTATION WITH ENID Cook. He placed one of his grandfather's journals on the desk. He could not help but notice that on one side of the desk was John Henning's binder and on the other was Enid's end-of-the-year report. He sat down in the swivel chair and looked out the windows across the square. Snow covered everything, making the most ordinary shapes look like confections. The square and the buildings around it could have been part of a Dickensian world. There was a solid majesty to the old buildings with icicles hanging from the eaves and Christmas decorations in the windows. It was almost as if Tiny Tim and his father might appear from around a corner at any minute. He rubbed his eyes and swiveled slowly around to the desk.

Will picked up John Henning's report, opened it, and began to read, but he realized when he was halfway down the first page that his mind had been elsewhere. He reread the page, but still couldn't focus on what was being said. He laced his fingers together behind his head, leaned back, and stared, unseeing, at the ceiling.

After fifteen or twenty minutes, he glanced at Enid Cook's books, sighed, and surrendered himself to his grandfather's journal. He held the smooth leather spine balanced on the palm of his hand, willing it to fall open to a page he should see. It fell open and Will began to read.

I cannot help but notice the closeness between Ruth and Will. It is almost as if Samuel has been reborn. I wish that I could develop that same closeness, the same rapport.

I try. I've vowed that I'll be there to support him whatever he decides to do. But, it seems that the closeness between us is lacking. If only Will understood, as I do, the bridge that connects us and yet keeps us apart.

I'd be lying to myself if I didn't admit that it hurts. I want to be as much a part of Will's life as Ruth has become. I sup-

pose I've made the same excuses all fathers have—work, civic
responsibilities, church all take time. Regardless, there is some-
thing missing between us. And I find myself unable to talk to
Ruth about it.

Will closed the book. *Oh, Grandpa,* he thought. His reverie was broken by the sound of the front door opening. Enid Cook turned on the lights in the front office and shook the snow from her coat. She looked mildly surprised when she saw him in his office. Quickly she hung up her coat and joined him.

"Mr. Martin. I'm glad to see you here so early. Perhaps we can go over the end-of-the-year report this morning." She glanced at the desktop. "Unless, of course, you're going to be busy reading that." She pointed her finger at John Henning's report.

"Miss Cook," Will said, trying to gather his wits. "Just between the two of us, what is it you don't like about Mr. Henning?"

"Mr. Martin, if you don't mind me saying so, he has no idea of the years it took your grandfather to build this company and its reputation. When you go back to New York I'm afraid he will destroy everything that this agency is known for!"

"Miss Cook, I think you feel the same way about me."

"With all due respect, when your grandfather founded this business his handshake was as good as his word. When your father, bless his soul, started working here, they were just like two peas in a pod. They worked side by side and they seemed to agree on everything."

"I've heard that before. Tell me about my father, Miss Cook. I was a small child, not quite four years old, when he and my mother died. I can hardly remember them. Tell me what you remember about him . . . please."

Enid cleared her throat and actually smiled. "Well, as I said he and your grandfather were very close and very much alike."

"Oh, how?"

"Well, they both thought that people were more important than protocol. They loved talking to people and helping people and they loved this agency." Enid's voice had softened. "They were good men."

"And if my father hadn't died he'd be your boss right now."

Enid looked at Will for a long moment and nodded her head. "I suppose."

Will thought for a moment of all the files he had sorted through the previous day, then he saw the Henning report on his desk and it brought him back to the present. "Miss Cook, I am keenly aware that I am not my grandfather. I come from a different time, a different era. I know how resistant this agency is to change, but change it must. I've hired John Henning to make those changes and I'm counting on you to get along with him."

"Mr. Martin, you are absolutely right. I knew your grandfather and you are not your grandfather." She turned on her heel and stomped out the door.

Will opened the journal and sifted through the pages. *Grandpa, why did you ever hire Enid Cook?*

14

THE FRONT OF MICK'S FLOWER SHOP WAS FESTOONED WITH BOUGHS OF PINE AND TINY, TWINKLING LIGHTS THREADED THROUGH THE PINE NEEDLES. A JOLLY FIVE-FOOT SANTA Claus holding a bouquet of red and white roses stood in the front window. When Will walked inside, the aroma of cinnamon and cloves enveloped him in a soothing cloud.

"Will!" Mick smiled as he wiped his hand on his pants. "What can I do for you?"

"A fellow like me can't pass up a bargain, Mick. Do you have another dozen roses at the Martin rate?"

"You bet! Do you want yellow roses again?"

"No, I think red this time."

Mick's smile widened. "Ah, not for your grandmother, then?"

Will shook his head. "No, for a friend."

"Miss Julia?" the florist asked, sliding back one of the cooler doors.

"Uh, no. Another friend." Will felt the color rise in his cheeks.

"Oh? Well, just a minute. I've got some fresher ones in the back. Do you want them in a box or a vase?"

"Put 'em in a vase, Mick," Will stammered.

"Coming right up."

Will wandered around the shop and found an arrangement that he thought might look nice above the fireplace in his grandmother's living room. As he stood deciding, Mick appeared with a crystal vase filled with roses, sprigs of baby's breath, and greenery. A Christmas bow was tied around the vase.

"This okay?" Mick asked, holding the vase for Will's inspection.

"Perfect! How much do I owe you?"

"Ten dollars," the older man said, beginning to pack the bottom of the vase in a cardboard holder, so it wouldn't tilt over in the car.

"But I need to pay for the vase," Will countered, opening his wallet.

"If the truth be known, Will, I ought to give you the flowers."

"I don't understand."

"I wouldn't be in business today if it weren't for your grandfather. Warren Martin lent me the money to buy this shop when no one else in town would give me the time of day. But I suppose you know all that."

Will gnawed on his lower lip. "No, I didn't, Mick. Maybe we could have lunch some time. I'd like to hear the whole story. But right now I'm late for an appointment."

"I understand. There's a good diner across the street. You stop by any time. I'd like to tell you what kind of a man your grandfather was." He took the ten dollars from Will and waved good-bye.

Will hopped into his car and pulled out into the swirls of snow. *Grandpa,* he thought, *it's just like you're two different people. The public good guy and this private man Gram and I didn't know existed.*

The Jaguar sped through town and pulled up in front of Renee's address. As Will climbed the steps to the apartment, the front door flew open.

"Hey, you're late," Justin shouted happily. Involuntarily Will glanced at his watch. It was five minutes after seven.

"Come in, Will, and let me take your coat," Renee said, laughing and tousling her young son's hair.

He handed her the vase of roses and a box of chocolate eclairs from his favorite bakery. "Merry Christmas, and thank you for inviting me."

"You shouldn't have," she smiled. "The roses are absolutely beautiful and I'm sure whatever is in this box will be yummy."

"Thank you."

"Dinner is ready, so please have a seat and Justin and I will be right back."

The little boy followed Renee into the kitchen and Will seated himself at the table and began looking around. It was a small but cozy apartment. A large framed Renoir print of ballet dancers was hung above the couch and a dozen pictures of Justin ranged along the mantel. A small, decorated Christmas tree stood on a table by the front window, near a fire of pine logs that burned in the fireplace.

Soon Justin returned with a basket full of hot rolls and plunked himself down in the chair next to Will. Renee carried in two plates and placed them in front of Will and Justin and then quickly returned with a third plate for herself.

"It looks wonderful," Will said appreciatively.

"Just your basic grilled chicken, mashed potatoes, and gravy," she replied, but she seemed pleased with his response and smiled as she bent over to help her son cut his meat.

"There's corn, too," Justin announced solemnly, and Will nodded as he sliced off a piece of chicken and placed it in his mouth.

"This is delicious," he said, and then turned his attention to Justin. "Have you been getting ready for Christmas?"

"Sort of, but mostly I've been studying dinosaurs."

"Oh, really?" Will said, taking a roll and passing the basket.

"Yup, I know every dinosaur's name by heart."

"So do I," Will teased.

"You don't, either," Justin said, shaking his head.

"Want to bet?"

Justin's eyes narrowed slightly, then he nodded his head. "Go ahead, name them."

Will looked at Renee with a twinkle in his eye and then began a recitation. "There's Stegosaurus, Apatosaurus—that used to be called Brontosaurus—Allosaurus, Lambeosaurus, Gorgosaurus, Plateosaurus, and the big boy, Tyrannosaurus, also known as T-rex."

Justin's mouth dropped open.

Will smiled at Renee, who had begun to laugh with delight. "And there's triceratops, protoceratops, pteranodon, dimetrodon, pterodactyl, Utahraptor, velociraptor, and ankylosaurus!"

Justin looked at Will intensely. "You done?"

"I think so."

"Parasaurolophus!" Justin shouted triumphantly.

Will hit the heel of his hand against his forehead. "How could I have forgotten that one?" he said.

"But you did pretty well," Justin admitted, taking a gulp of milk and wiping his mouth with his napkin.

"Thanks. Coming from you that's a compliment."

"Bedtime, tiger," Renee said after Justin had finished his second chocolate eclair. "But help me clean off the table first."

"Ah, Mom."

"I'll help," Will said. "I'm pretty good at clearing tables."

Justin smiled at his mother. "Thanks," he said, turning to Will, "I needed a break," and then scampered off to get ready for bed, leaving the adults laughing.

A few minutes later Renee and Will stood side by side in the kitchen. She was washing and he was drying. "You really didn't have to help me with this," she said.

"No problem. My grandma trained me right."

They finished putting the last of the dishes away and entered the living room just as Justin bounded into the room wearing a pair of Jurassic Park pajamas. "You know the biggest problem with these pajamas?" he asked.

"What?" Will asked, turning him around, taking in all of the dinosaurs.

"Most of the dinosaurs are Cretaceous," said the six-year-old.

Will reached out and shook Justin's hand. "Thanks for a great dinner, Justin."

"Thanks for coming, Will." The small boy kissed his mother good night and scooted out of the room.

Will and Renee sat facing each other on the couch. "Did you find a gift for your grandmother?" she asked.

"Well, I found a gift my grandfather had purchased, but I'm not sure it was for my grandmother."

"Oh?" Renee pulled her knees up and wrapped her arms around her legs. "Why don't you tell me about it."

"I don't know quite where to start." Will rubbed the bridge of his nose.

"Why not at the beginning."

For the next half hour Will explained the entry in his grandfather's journal that had started his quest. He finished by saying, "I'm running out of ideas. I've talked to quite a number of people who knew Grandpa. I spent half of yesterday going through boxes of old records. I've been trying to find clues in his journals. So far, nothing."

"Have you read all of them?" Renee's concern was comforting to him.

Will shook his head. "It's a huge stack, Renee."

"Keep looking. I'm sure what you need is in one of those books. But even if you don't find what you're looking for, I can tell you there were never two more devoted people than your grandmother and grandfather. You've got to know that."

"I know, I know. But when Mr. Taylor brought out that emerald . . . I mean, I just can't figure who he bought it for. You ought to see it. Whoever he meant it for must have been awfully special to him. I can't explain it, but when he said it was a May birthstone it was just like he'd driven a knife into me."

"Have faith. There's a logical explanation, I'm sure of it."

Will smiled. "Some people I know wouldn't share your confidence."

Renee reached over and patted his hand. "Will, it's going to be all right. How is your grandmother handling all of this?"

"Oh, she puts on a good front most of the time, but I can tell this has really gotten to her. Until all this came up she felt there hadn't been any secrets between them. Learning something like this after he's gone, after there's no way to talk it through . . . well . . ."

Suddenly Renee snapped her fingers. "Maybe there's something I can do. Your grandfather gave all the employees one of those privately printed desk calendars with thoughts for the day. It was sort of an office tradition. I've always said I was going to get around to organizing those thoughts."

"So?"

"Well, he chose the thoughts himself—he wrote a few, I believe, and they really made you think. I kept all of them. They're stuck away in the bottom of my dresser drawer. I could go through them and see if there are any clues to Lillian."

"It's probably a long shot, but that would be great," he said, as he rose to his feet. "Well, it's late, I'd better leave before I overstay my welcome."

Will followed Renee to the front closet and let her help him into his coat. "Thanks for dinner, it was great. And thanks for listening. You're an easy person to talk to."

Renee looked into Will's face. "I'm glad you came. I'll try to get to those calendars tomorrow."

Will walked slowly down the steps to his car. Large flakes of snow drifted down on his head, and he looked up and stuck out his tongue to catch a flake. He didn't notice Renee watching him from her front window.

15

Ruth Martin let the bag full of Christmas gifts hang from one hand while she signaled for a taxi with the other. The cab pulled up in front of the department store that faced the town square and the driver jumped out and opened the rear door. "Afternoon, Mrs. Martin," he said cheerfully.

"Good afternoon, Andrew. It's good to see you again. I didn't know you were driving a taxi."

"I'm just helping my uncle during the holidays. My last final was Friday and I don't have to be back at the university until the tenth of January. Seemed like a win—win situation. Uncle Lloyd never has enough drivers at this time of the year, and I can use the extra cash next semester."

"Well, it's good to see you. You look well." Ruth adjusted herself in the back seat of the cab and Andrew pulled into traffic.

"I was so sorry when your husband died last summer," Andrew said, looking in his rear-view mirror. "He was a good man."

"Thank you. I've always believed so, too," Gram said.

"You know, he was instrumental in helping me get this scholarship I have."

"Oh? I'm not sure I knew about that," Ruth said, leaning forward slightly.

The young man glanced in the mirror again. "I'm not sure exactly how he did it. I mean, my grades were okay, but they weren't spectacular. But Mr. Martin wrote a letter to the dean of the college and before you know it, I've got a full scholarship. Pays for all my tuition and books. I would never have been able to go to college full-time without it. He was a great guy."

"Yes, he was," Ruth agreed.

"I'm the first one from my family to ever go to college, and I'll be the first one in the whole Hoggard family to ever graduate. And all because of your husband."

"I'm sure he'd be proud of you, Andrew."

They rode the rest of the way in silence. The cab pulled up in front of the Martin residence. "That's nine dollars and twenty-five cents," Andrew Hoggard said, as he opened the back door of the taxi.

Ruth handed him a twenty-dollar bill. "Keep the change, Andrew, and good luck with college."

"Thanks," he called out, as he pulled away from the curb.

Ruth turned to start up the front steps when she heard a voice yelling from the backyard. "The crowd cheers wildly as the batter steps into the box."

Gram's forehead wrinkled. "What in the world is Will up to?" she whispered as she made her way down the driveway.

"There's the pitch and a line drive down the left field. It drops just short of the wall for a double."

Gram turned the corner of the house in time to see Will throw another snow-dusted pine cone into the air and attack it with a baseball bat. "Martin enters the box," he called out.

"Here comes the pitch. It's a slider. Martin gets his body into this one and it's over the wall for a home run!" The pine cone sailed over the fence.

Will threw both arms in the air in an exultant gesture and began dancing in a circle. Suddenly he spotted his grandmother, and his face turned bright red.

"Quite a game. Who's winning?"

"I am," he smiled. "Knocked a good dozen over the wall. I hope Mrs. Perkins doesn't complain too much. Been Christmas shopping?"

"Well, a bit." She held up the bag she was carrying. "I decided it was time to get out and about a little more. I stopped at the Golden Dragon and had lunch.

"Good for you, Gram." They turned and walked together toward the back door.

"I didn't expect to find you at home," she said.

"I was getting too tense. I'm tired of working six days a week and getting so little done. So I came home, and while I was putting on my grubbies I spotted my old bat," he shrugged.

She shifted the shopping bag to her other hand. "Well, it looks like you haven't lost your touch. You used to spend hours out here swinging at pine cones."

"It took me back a few years, that's for sure. Here, let me carry that." Will reached for the bag.

"Not so fast, nosy. I can carry it myself." The two of them entered the kitchen.

"You know, Gram, it made me think of those times Grandpa used to throw a ball to me. It used to surprise me that he could throw a curve as well as he did."

"Oh, really?"

"Uh huh. I got so I could hit it about nine times out of ten. When I started playing college ball there were darn few pitchers who could get a curve past me."

"You always did have a good swing. Well, I'm glad you were having some fun just now. You deserve it. I've been a little worried about you."

"I guess I haven't been much fun to be around."

"I can understand your being a little down, what with everything that's going on in your life," she replied.

"Guess I'll go put the bat away." Will climbed the stairs and started down the hallway toward his room when he paused in front of his grandfather's den. Tentatively he reached out and took hold of the knob. He pushed the door open and stood examining his grandfather's hideaway. Nothing had been moved since his unexpected death. Will propped the bat against the wall and walked to the old roll-top desk. His fingers traced the leather desk pad and stroked the gold Cross pen. He slid open the middle drawer and looked at the monogrammed stationery.

He sat down and began opening other drawers. In the top right-hand one he found a pair of rimless bifocals. He put them on and squinted around the room as he turned in the swivel chair. As the open doorway came into view he saw a blurred figure standing there. Startled, he took off the glasses. "Gram!" he said.

"You scared me half to death, Will."

"The feeling's mutual. I thought you were downstairs."

"I just came up to put these gifts in a safe place. I can't believe how much you look like Warren in those glasses."

Will laughed nervously. "Oh, Gram."

"No, really. When your grandfather was your age he looked just like you."

"Enid Cook says she sees no resemblance." He smiled wanly.

"I'd say you're the spitting image. It's uncanny. When I saw you sitting there it gave me quite a start. What were you doing in here?"

"Just looking around. You don't mind, do you?"

"Of course not." She turned to leave. "Oh, by the way, you did remember that tonight is the Christmas Ball, didn't you?"

"Of course," said Will, although his face clearly showed that he had completely forgotten. "Why don't you come with me? It's going to be the event of the year, according to Julia."

"I'm sure it will be," his grandmother replied. "But I'm quite tired."

"Are you sure? We could leave early." Will was surprised to hear a pleading tone in his voice.

"Looking for an excuse? I'd think you'd want to spend the night with Julia."

"I suppose," Will said. "Anyway, I still have a couple of hours until I have to put on my tuxedo."

"I guess you'll be eating there," Ruth said as she turned to leave.

"I suppose," he replied. Will turned back to the desk and opened another drawer. Inside were several photograph albums. He lifted the top one out and began examining the pictures. Warren Martin had been a precise man. Each photograph had a date and a location written on the back. Will slid a picture of a small baby from its mounting corners, turned it over, and read, *Samuel Martin, six days old.* He turned the photograph over and looked at his father. He turned the pages, watching his father grow up. In the second album were pictures of his father and mother on their wedding day. A lump formed in his throat as he looked at the pictures of these happy, handsome people he could barely remember.

The hours slipped by as Will looked through two boxes of memorabilia from past trips and examined everything in the desk. Finally, a small framed picture caught his attention. It showed Will and his grandfather at the lake. Will remembered the day, remembered holding the first fish he'd ever caught. The picture was more than twenty-five years old. He cradled it in his hands.

"Will," his grandmother called. "You're due at the Christmas Ball in thirty minutes."

"Thanks, Gram." He looked around at the mess he'd created. "I'll clean up this room tomorrow. Don't worry about it."

"That's fine," she called from the kitchen.

As Will placed the picture back on the desk, he felt the back of the frame move under his thumb. He turned it over and slid out the picture. Beneath it was a second picture.

This one showed three people: his grandfather, another man, and a woman between them. Both men had their arms around the woman. Slowly Will removed the photograph and turned it over. On the back, in a feminine hand, was written, *Warren, thanks for having me along. Love L.* He looked at the photograph again, staring at the woman's pleasant face. "Lillian," he said in awe, as he shoved the photograph into his pocket, "I've found you."

16

WILL HANDED THE KEYS TO HIS CAR TO
THE PARKING ATTENDANT AT THE CALDWELL
COUNTRY CLUB. THE NIGHT WAS CRISP AND
CLEAR. A FULL MOON HAD RISEN OVER THE
mountains to the east, bathing the frosty snow-covered
lawn in light. Ice crystals formed halos around the lights in
the parking lot. He buttoned his tuxedo jacket and stepped
into the foyer of the country club. A hat-check girl in an
abbreviated Santa Claus suit took his topcoat. "Merry
Christmas," she smiled.

Will smiled back. "Merry Christmas." He made his way into the ballroom and spotted Julia surrounded by a group of people. She was dressed in a royal-blue velvet gown and had a sparkling tiara in her blond hair. Will waved discreetly in her direction and Julia said something to the people in her circle and quickly made her way across the room, a smile frozen on her face.

"Julia," he said, pulling the picture from his pocket, "take a look at this."

"Take a look at what?" she replied sharply. "You're nearly half an hour late."

"I know, I'm sorry, but I have a good reason. You aren't going to believe this." Will could barely contain himself. "It's her picture!"

Julia looked completely confused. "Whose picture, Will?"

"Lillian. I've found Lillian!"

"Beautiful evening, Julia," a woman in a low-cut evening gown purred as she glided by.

"Thank you, Caroline," Julia said, smiling. She turned to Will and the smile faded. "Forget about it for one night! This is the Christmas Ball."

Will tried to get Julia to look at the picture, but she turned away. "I don't think you know what this means. This is amazing."

"Put that picture away, Will," she commanded through clenched teeth.

"But . . ."

"Put it away!" Suddenly her face lit up in a smile. "Oh, Mr. Carlisle," Julia called, pulling Will through the crowd. "I want you to meet him," she whispered, tightening her grip on his arm. "He's someone you need to know, his law firm is the biggest in the Northeast."

"How wonderful," Will replied under his breath.

Will was impressed with how well the evening had been planned. A sumptuous buffet was provided, and people balanced plates in their hands while consuming considerable quantities of shrimp, chicken, and steak. A fifteen-piece band played old Tommy Dorsey hits, and couples swayed. Those who had enjoyed the tulip-shaped glasses of champagne swayed perhaps more than others. As the night progressed, the crowd began to thin.

"Aren't you Will Martin?" asked a rotund man with a walrus mustache.

"Yes," replied Will. "You have me at a disadvantage."

"I'm Grant Summerson and this is Ida, my wife."

Will shook the outstretched hand and nodded to Mrs. Summerson. "I'm pleased to meet you."

"We knew your grandfather from the time we first moved to this town."

"Back in nineteen forty-eight," his wife added.

"You must feel settled in," Will said.

"More settled some days than others," Grant Summerson teased.

"But well preserved," Ida laughed.

"Anyway, we found our way to your grandfather's real estate agency back then and Warren Martin took us under his wing. He found us our first house."

"I hope you were well treated."

Both the Summersons nodded in unison. "Oh, my yes. In those days Martin Real Estate was just your grandfather and his secretary, Miss Cook. We loved the home he found for us," said Ida.

"Hated to move," Grant added. "But when our family grew we finally had to find a bigger place. Went right back to Martin Real Estate."

"That was in nineteen sixty-six," Ida chimed in.

"I'm glad my grandfather treated you well," said Will.

"Absolutely. We still live in that house. When you find someone you can trust, you stay with him," said Grant. "Your grandfather knew how to treat a customer."

"So people tell me," smiled Will. He reached into his jacket pocket. "Could I ask you two a question?" The Summersons nodded. "You've known my grandfather for a long time. Do either of you recognize the other two people in this photograph?"

Grant stared at the picture for a moment, then shook his head. He handed the photograph to his wife. Ida studied it, then said, "I'm sorry, I don't know either of those folks. Probably folks he met on one of his fishing trips."

"Ah, there you are, Will," Julia said, grabbing his elbow. "How are you this evening?" she asked the Summersons, as she pushed Will away from the couple. "Please excuse us a moment."

"Of course, my dear. This is a fabulous ball, you are to be congratulated."

"Nice meeting you," Will called, before the Summersons disappeared from sight.

Julia led him across the dance floor to a relatively private corner.

"You want to dance?" he said with a smile.

"Not on your life!" she crackled. "Put that picture away!"

Will slipped the photograph he'd been holding into his pocket.

"And leave it there. Don't you understand what a fool you're making of yourself?"

"In what way?" His cheeks were flushed and his teeth felt like they might disintegrate from the pressure of his jaw.

Julia clenched fists and blew out her breath. "It is bad enough that your grandfather had an affair, but why show the evidence to every single person in this country club?"

"I'm trying to find out if anyone here knows who these people are. That's all. They have no idea that anything may have been going on between my grandfather and the woman. Besides, Christmas is coming fast, and I intend to give my grandmother the gift she wants."

"Will, trust me, this is not a Christmas gift that anyone wants. Get her something else, anything else. Finding this woman will do no one any good, not you or your grand-mother."

Will looked at Julia's beautiful face. Not one strand of her hair was out of place. He reached out and took hold of both her hands. "You really don't understand how impor-tant this is to me, do you?"

"No, I don't. I think this search is the most absurd thing I've ever heard of. And I'm not sure I really want to know any more about it."

Will turned away, stung. "You won't have to, Julia. I'm sorry if I've ruined your evening. I think you and I have dif-ferent priorities."

"What do you mean?" She put her hand on his arm and he turned to look at her.

"You want things that I'm not interested in, like a high-flying social life and influential friends. I'm just trying to be truthful, Julia. You're a nice woman and a beautiful woman, but we'd never be happy, and more than likely we'd be mis-erable." Will turned and walked back across the dance floor. Julia followed him for a moment, anger obvious on her face. Then she took a deep breath to calm herself and the smile returned as the crowd flowed around her and she once more became part of it.

Will tipped the Santa girl and retrieved his coat. He took one last look at Julia across the dance floor and walked out the door. He handed the valet his claim ticket and waited by the front door for his car to appear.

Absentmindedly he fingered the picture in his pocket. He took it out and inspected the three figures standing there. He tapped it against his hand as his car slid up to the curb. He tipped the valet and drove quietly through the moon-drenched night. The Jag seemed to have a mind of its own, and before long he pulled up in front of Renee Carr's apartment. Although it was after eleven o'clock, a light was still burning in her window.

"This is absurd," he said to himself as he climbed out of the car. Will stopped on the sidewalk and stared at the window. He shook his head and started to get back in the car when the apartment door opened.

"All dressed up and nowhere to go?" Renee asked from the open doorway.

Will smiled and began walking up the steps. "It was the Christmas Ball at the country club tonight. I made an appearance, but . . . you know."

"Want to come in?"

"It's pretty late. Are you sure?"

Renee shivered slightly. "You might as well. You're here now, and it's warmer inside."

Will thanked her, and the two of them walked inside and sat down on the couch.

"What brings a nice guy like you out on a night like this?" Renee asked warmly.

"I . . ." Will stammered, looking for an excuse, "I wondered if you'd looked at the calendars."

"Not yet. I had a full day of lessons today, but soon. Cross my heart."

Will nodded. "Thanks. I really don't mean to rush you."

Renee looked at him curiously. "What's the matter, Will?"

He reached into the pocket of his tuxedo and withdrew the photograph. "I found this picture in my grandfather's study today." He turned it over. "Read what it says on the back." He handed Renee the picture. "Do you know who they are?"

Renee put the photograph under the table lamp. "Your grandfather, of course, and Fred Askew. He runs a fishing camp. Your grandfather went fishing there nearly every summer, but I don't know who the woman is. I'm sorry."

Will looked at her with amazement. "You know who he is! You're incredible. Do you know where his fishing camp is? Does he still run it?"

"Will, I haven't had anything to do with your grandfather since I got . . . well, for several years. I have no idea whether he continued his relationship with Mr. Askew, but they were good friends once. Your grandfather used to have a photograph of the two of them on his desk."

"I know if I can find Fred Askew, he can lead me to Lillian and I can fulfill my grandmother's wish."

"Is it just for your grandmother? Or are you doing this for you?"

Will shrugged. "Both of us, I guess. You know, Renee, everyone I talk to paints this picture of Grandpa as the per-

fect man and for years that's the same picture I've had of
him. Then, suddenly, I find this other side that I can't rec-
oncile with the man I knew. It's almost like Jekyll and Hyde.
I've got to find Lillian so I can make sense of this puzzle."

He slipped the picture back in his jacket.

"Let me see what I can do to locate Fred Askew. I'm
beginning to realize how important this is to you. Now
you'd better scoot. It is very late and I do have an early
class." She opened the door for him and they stood there
looking at each other for a long moment. He reached out
and took her hands in his. He felt the strength and the soft-
ness. She gave his hands a gentle squeeze.

"Thanks, Renee." He walked down the steps and drove
away.

17

THE WORLD SEEMED SOMEWHAT LIGHTER
A FEW MORNINGS LATER AS WILL SAT IN
THE SWIVEL CHAIR. ALREADY HE'D WORKED
HIS WAY THROUGH A DOZEN OR MORE OF
the folders that lay on his desk. He glanced at his watch.
Barely nine o'clock. He turned in his chair and looked out
across the square. Throngs of people were on the street, the
stores were decorated in their holiday finery, and big, white
flakes of snow were falling softly. *It looks like a Christmas card,*
he thought. He smiled at the scene and started to turn back

to the desk when he spotted Renee Carr's ancient Chevrolet pulling up to the curb across the street. His smile broadened.

Renee gathered a shopping bag from the back seat and walked briskly across the street to Martin Real Estate. She stood in front of the building for a moment as if inspecting it, then opened the door and walked in. "And how is Janice Harr?" she said cheerfully as the door closed behind her.

"Renee! It's so good to see you. It has been ages."

"Too long," replied Renee.

"And how is Justin doing? He's such a bright little boy."

"Still bright. Sometimes a little scary, but he's fine."

"Growing like a weed, I'll bet," said Mrs. Harr.

Renee nodded her head in agreement.

"I always felt a special bond between us, you being a Carr and me being a Harr," said the older woman.

Renee smiled. "There but for a consonant go I." Both women chuckled. She patted Mrs. Harr on the shoulder and started to walk toward Will's office, but Enid Cook intercepted her.

"Renee Carr," said the older woman, "you're a sight for sore eyes." The two of them hugged briefly. "Oh, I do wish you'd come back to the agency."

"They were good days, Enid, but I'm very happy doing what I'm doing, and it gives me more time with Justin."

"And how is my favorite boy?"

"He's fine. Totally absorbed in dinosaurs at the moment."
She smiled. "Is Will . . . that is, is Mr. Martin available?"

At that moment she turned to see Will lounging against
the open door of his office. "Miss Carr," he said with a
grin. "Come in, come in."

"Can you work me into your schedule?"

"Of course, of course, I'm delighted to see you. Come in."

Renee entered Will's office and slowly turned completely
around. "Just like when your grandfather was here."

"Well, some changes are in the offing, for better or
worse." He pulled up a chair to the side of the desk. "Have
a seat."

Renee inspected the desktop. "You're missing something.
Where's your nameplate?"

"My what?"

She pointed at the desk. "You need a nameplate."

"Why? My name's on the door."

"Where did you put your grandfather's?"

"I didn't put it anywhere," Will said, shaking his head.
"Maybe Miss Cook stored it for safekeeping. She seems to
store everything else."

Renee stood up. "Mind if I look in the desk?"

"Go right ahead," Will said, laughing softly.

In the bottom left-hand drawer she found what she was
looking for. She held up the block of oak with a shiny
brass nameplate. Renee walked to the credenza beneath a
wall covered with pictures and citations and placed the

nameplate on it. She returned to her chair and inspected her work.

"Does that bring back memories?"

"Uh huh. I loved working here."

"Then why did you leave?" he asked.

"I had a chance to start my own business ... the dance studio."

"Do you like it? Is it all you hoped it would be?" Will asked.

"Pretty much. I've wanted to dance since I was half Justin's size. My dream was to join the Joffrey."

Will rested his chin in his hand. "And did you get there?"

Renee shook her head and her reddish brown shoulder-length hair swirled around her face. "Nope. Skied into a tree when I was sixteen and damaged my knee," she said, pointing out the window toward the mountains.

"That's too bad," Will said sympathetically.

Renee drew her arms around herself and stared out the window. "I thought so, too, for a while. Then I started working for your grandfather. Years passed, but not the desire to dance. He caught me crying one day, when I was feeling sorry for myself. He made me tell him what was wrong and by the time I was through, I'd told him everything about my ambitions. I remember he gave me his big white handkerchief and said, 'When God closes one door he always opens another.'"

She turned from the window and looked into Will's eyes. "A few months later the top floor of the shoe store became vacant and your grandfather took me over to see it. I thought he just wanted my opinion about the retail value of the place, but he told me it was mine if I wanted it—for a very reasonable rent."

She grew thoughtful. "Anyway, it was he who encouraged me to start the dance studio, to pass my talents on to others. It was tough at first. No one knew about me and I had just a handful of students. But my clientele has grown and today I'm as happy as I've ever been," she said, smiling broadly.

Will nodded.

"Unless, of course, you raise the rent," she teased him.

"I doubt I'll do that," he replied.

"And what about you?"

"What about me?"

"You've come home and started learning about this agency, but you're going to pack up and head back to New York the first chance you get, right?"

Will rubbed his chin. "I guess so, at least that's what I've been planning to do, but lately . . ."

". . . Lately what?"

"Oh, I don't know. I'd forgotten how this place grows on you."

Renee lowered her eyes to the desktop. "Yes, it does."

A flicker of a smile crossed his lips. He liked this woman. She was smart and strong and very attractive. "Did you just drop in to chat?" he said at last.

"No, no. I brought the calendars." She reached into the shopping bag and dropped them onto the already cluttered desktop.

"And?"

"And I just skimmed through them." Her eyes twinkled. "But I did find this." She flipped open one of the calendar pads to a page she had marked with a slip of paper. She pointed to a note written in pencil.

"Mr. Martin's annual fishing trip. Edenton Lake."

"It's in the July nineteen eighty-nine calendar," Renee added.

"Is there a phone number scribbled on there anywhere?" Will asked.

"No, but it did jog my memory. Fred Askew ran a fishing camp at Edenton Lake."

Will reached in his bottom drawer for the phone directory. "You don't know the area code, by chance?"

"Sorry, no."

Will flipped through the pages of the directory. "Here it is, four-one-two. Let's see if directory assistance can give us a number."

Renee looked at her watch and stood up. "I have to run. I have a class of students waiting. I didn't realize the time."

"Do you have a busy day?"

"Sort of. This is my half day of work. One of the commitments I made to Justin when I started my own business was our weekly date. Every Thursday I pick him up after school and we do something special."

"Sounds smart," Will said, grinning.

"Your grandfather suggested it. He said you had to put everything in perspective. No success outside the home matters without a good family life."

"Sounds like a sterling philosophy. Say 'hi' to Justin for me."

Renee nodded. "Take your time with the calendars, and good luck."

"Thanks, you've been a great help."

Renee waved good-bye and walked quickly out of the building, stopping only to say a few parting words to Enid and Janice Harr.

Will turned his attention to finding Fred Askew. He picked up the phone and dialed Information.

"Thank you for calling directory assistance. City, please."

"Edenton Lake."

"One moment, please. Which listing?"

"Fred Askew."

There was a brief pause. "I have a Frederick Askew."

"That's probably the one," Will said.

"Hold for the number." A computerized voice came on the line, and gave him 412-655-4012.

Will wrote the number on his desk pad. He placed the receiver in its cradle, then almost immediately picked it up again. He punched in the numbers and the phone in

Edenton Lake began to ring. "Seven . . . eight . . . nine . . . ten." Will counted the rings and finally replaced the phone.

He returned to the work at hand, pausing every hour or so to dial the number at Edenton Lake without success. *So near, and yet so far*, he thought. He looked at his watch. One-thirty. He'd worked right through lunch. Suddenly an idea seized him.

He jumped up and walked into John Henning's office. "John, something's come up. I need to be gone for the rest of the day. Think you can handle it?"

John Henning smiled. "You can count on it." He turned back to his laptop as Will left his office.

Will filled the Jaguar with gas and cleaned out the car. At five minutes to two, he headed for Renee's dance studio. She was just locking the front door as he pulled into the parking lot.

He punched the button and the window rolled down. "Renee," he called.

"Yes?" she said, puzzled, but pleased to see him.

"What are you and Justin planning for today?"

"We have some Christmas shopping to do." She opened the door of her car and threw in her gym bag. "Why?"

"Well, apparently Fred Askew still lives up at Edenton Lake, but I can't get him to answer the phone. I'm going to drive up there and see if I can find him. I was hoping you and Justin might want to come along."

A smile flickered across Renee's face, then she shook her head. "I'm sorry, we can't."

"I know I should have given you more warning, but the idea just popped into my head. Besides, I can't show him a photograph over the phone."

"I don't think so, Will." She started to climb into her car.

"Okay, I'm sorry it didn't work out," Will said, puzzled. "I was just hoping."

Renee got back out of her car and walked slowly to the Jaguar. "Will, let me try to explain. Today the mother of one of my students was talking about the Christmas Ball the other night."

"Oh?" said Will.

"She knows everything that goes on in this town . . . and, well, Miss Welsch is a lovely woman."

Will climbed slowly out of his car. "Renee, I've dated Julia Welsch a few times. But that relationship has ended. Besides, we're not going on a date, we're going on a trip."

A smile played on Renee's lips. "Well, when you put it that way. Justin has never seen Edenton Lake."

"Then let's go get him." Will walked around the car and opened the door for Renee.

"Just a minute," she said, as she returned to her car and locked the door.

The Jaguar pulled out of the parking lot. "This is quite a nice car, Will," Renee said, stroking the leather seat with the tips of her fingers.

"Thanks. It gets you where you're going and then some. Which way?"

"Take a left at the next corner. Justin's school is about six blocks down on the right." She looked at the digital clock on the dashboard. "He's getting out of school just about now."

Justin was standing in front of the school as the silver Jaguar pulled up. Renee rolled down her window. "Want to go on an adventure, sweetheart?"

Justin's eyes became enormous and he smiled from ear to ear as he climbed into the back seat of the car. "Is this your car, Will?"

Will nodded. "Hi, Justin."

"It's cool."

The engine hummed as they began the two-hour drive to Edenton Lake.

"Can I ask you a question?" Justin asked, squirming against his seat belt.

"Sure," Will replied.

"Do you know which dinosaur had two brains?"

Renee smiled at Will. "You're the one to blame. Show-off."

Will looked in the rear-view mirror and saw Justin smiling back at him. "Stegosaurus," he said.

"I guess that was too easy," the boy replied.

Will nodded. "Pretty easy."

Justin scratched his head. "Okay, which one would be a good railroad worker?"

Will smiled at Renee. "I don't know, Justin. Which dinosaur would be a good railroad worker?"

"Triceratops, 'cause he has spikes on his tail."

Will whistled appreciatively. "Did you make that up yourself, Justin?"

The boy nodded.

"Not bad for a six-year-old."

"He's a little scary," his mother replied.

Justin fell asleep in the back seat and Renee and Will drove along for miles in companionable silence, watching the snow-covered woods sweep by.

"I'm hungry. Are we going to stop for dinner?" Justin whined, waking in an irritable mood.

"It won't be much longer till we get to the lake, honey."

"I'm hungry now," he said emphatically.

Renee turned in her seat and gave her son a stern look.

"Actually, I'm kind of hungry, too," Will said, looking for an exit sign.

Justin bounced in the back seat. "You're outvoted, Mom."

"Don't you guys think you can gang up on me," Renee smiled.

Will pulled off the highway and into a roadside McDonald's, and Justin gave him a high-five as he climbed from the car.

18

THE REMAINS OF THE CHICKEN McNUGGETS LAY IN THEIR CARDBOARD CONTAINER AS JUSTIN SLID INTO A POOL OF PLASTIC BALLS, BURNING OFF SOME OF THE ENERGY HE HAD stored during the car ride. Renee and Will sat at a red-topped table sipping hot chocolate and watching him. "He's quite the boy," Will said, laughing.

"Yes, he is." Renee studied Will's face.

He sipped his chocolate slowly, and started to say something, but stopped.

"Something bothering you, Mr. Martin?"

Will kept looking at the boy. "Not really. Just curious."

"Oh? About what?"

Will turned to look at Renee across the table. "I was wondering about Justin's father."

Renee cocked her head to one side and pressed her lips together in a wan smile.

"You don't have to answer . . ."

"No problem. At least now it isn't." She took another sip of her hot chocolate. "I . . . we haven't seen him in over three years, since just after the divorce. He's working for a computer company in Paris."

Will nodded his head, slowly.

"It's for the best. Gary was so obsessed with his work he never had time for Justin—or me."

"I was four when I lost my father," Will said, quietly. "It's a hard thing to go through."

"That's the only thing I'm sorry about. Justin has never really known what it's like to have a father. As far as my relationship with Gary goes, we're both much better off this way."

"What makes you say that?"

"Oh, you know, you put on such a show while you're dating. Then you get married and . . . well, he turned out to be very different from the person I thought he was during our courtship. I suppose I was different, too. Anyway, you make choices in life. Sometimes you make the wrong ones. God gave us that responsibility. I used to blame Him for what happened, then I realized that I, not God, had made the choice to marry Gary. So I decided to learn from that mistake and move on. It has made me much more careful, I can tell you."

"I think I understand," Will said, softly.

Renee looked past Will toward the play area. "It was nice to visit the agency today," she said, changing the subject. "At least those memories are good ones."

"It was good having you there. It was easy to see that you felt right at home. I couldn't believe how Enid Cook greeted you. I've never even seen her give a hint of a smile since I arrived and suddenly she's smiling so broadly I wasn't sure who she was."

"Oh, Will. She's a great lady."

"Well, she's set in her ways and I don't think she has much good to say about me," he replied.

"Considering what she's gone through, I really admire her."

"You do?" Will's brow wrinkled. "Tell me about her."

Renee toyed with her cup and watched Justin climb energetically up a rope ladder. "Didn't your grandfather ever talk about what went on at work?"

Will shook his head. "Maybe that's why I'm having such a tough time getting a grip on how best to run the agency. He was a very private man, my grandfather. Tell me what you know, please."

"Will, I'm not much for gossip."

"I'm just trying to find out why Enid's so . . . so distant. I'm sure I have no interest in titillating details." Will raised his eyes skyward.

"This is pretty serious," she said, quietly.

He sensed the tension in her voice. "I'm sorry. Please, go on."

Renee took a deep breath. "When Enid was younger she was quite an attractive woman. However, both of her parents became invalids before she turned twenty. They needed . . . demanded all of her free time. She closed herself off from the rest of the world by spending years caring for them. Her parents and Martin Real Estate became her world. She never dated, never got away from the house except to go to work. Then her father required extensive surgery. He had no insurance and the medical bills were overwhelming." Renee looked into Will's troubled face.

"I'm beginning to see the picture," he said quietly.

"She became depressed. There just didn't seem to be a light at the end of the tunnel. And in that time of despair she did what she felt she had to do. She borrowed ten thousand dollars from the agency."

"What do you mean, she borrowed the money?"

"She took what she had to have."

Will stared open-mouthed at Renee. "You mean Enid Cook embezzled ten thousand dollars?"

Renee nodded as she warmed her hands around the cup of hot chocolate.

"There are a lot of things I might have expected, but that wasn't one of them."

"It cast a pall over the whole agency. Like I said, I'm not much of one for gossip, but the story spread. Quite frankly, I had mixed emotions. All of us were appalled at what she'd done, but we were worried, too. What was going to become of her and her parents? We knew how your grandfather valued honesty, and it was obvious she'd violated his trust and he'd have to let her go."

"But she's still here," Will said, his brow furrowed.

"Thanks to your grandfather. I never heard a word from him about what had happened, but someone paid off all the family expenses and Enid Cook became the firm's accountant."

Will shook his head. "Why? Why on earth would he put her in charge of the money? I have to admit, my grandfather confuses me at times."

"It confused me too, at first. But then I began to realize how wise your grandfather was. Do you think there has ever been one dime that hasn't been accounted for since her promotion?" Renee shook her head. "Enid can tell you where every cent has gone. You see, by promoting her he helped her grow, and it's obvious he completely forgave her. He had an uncanny ability to recognize why people acted the way they did and he knew how to help them get over the rough spots in the road."

"It's still hard to figure out, Renee."

"Hi, Will . . . Mom," Justin panted, running up. "Did you see me hanging upside down?" he asked proudly.

"Yes, honey. You are very agile."

"Through?" Will asked Renee. She nodded and handed him the empty cup. Will dumped the tray in the garbage can and they headed back to the car.

Snow was falling harder as they continued on their way to Edenton Lake, the Jaguar gripping the road firmly. They drove in silence as Will wrestled with what he'd learned about Enid Cook and his grandfather, and Justin fell asleep again.

By the time they reached the lake the snow had stopped and the clouds were sliding past, revealing patches of blue. Will pulled up to the general store. "I'll go see if I can get directions to Askew's place," he whispered to Renee. "I'll leave the car running so you don't get cold."

The inside of the general store smelled strongly of leather and Neatsfoot oil. Two elderly gentlemen were playing checkers near a wood-burning stove. As Will entered, one of them rose. "Now, don'tcha even think about cheatin'," he said to the other man. "What can I do for ya', mister?" he asked, stroking his beard.

"I'm looking for Fred Askew's place."

"Oh? Whatcha need?"

Will was a little uncertain how to continue. "He, well, he and my grandfather used to fish together and . . . well, it's kind of a long story."

"Who was your granddad?" the bearded man asked, the curiosity sparkling in his eyes.

"Warren Martin."

"You're Warren Martin's grandson?" The old man's eyes lit up. "Then you must be Will." He thrust out his hand.

"That's right," Will replied, confused but pleased.

"Your granddad used to talk about you every summer when he came here fishing with old Fred. He sure was proud of you."

"I had no idea," Will stammered.

"Fred'll be glad to see you, my boy." The old man scratched his whiskers. "How well do ya' know the territory?"

"Not very well."

"Let me draw you a map." The old man retrieved a piece of paper from beneath the counter and the stub of a pencil from behind his ear. "This here's the main road," he said, drawing a line. "Keep on going about half a mile till you come to a sign that says MONROE BASIN ROAD. Take that road until you see the lake through the trees. Fred's cabin's the one on the left side of the road. There's a sign above the front porch says ASKEW INN." The old man cackled. "Can't miss it."

"Thanks," Will said, picking up the piece of paper. "I appreciate the help."

"Nice to make your acquaintance." The old man sat back down at the checkerboard. "Charlie! I said no cheatin'."

Will hurried back to the car. "It's just a little further," he said, as he slipped into the warm interior. Justin stirred in the back seat.

In a little less than five minutes they pulled up in front of Fred Askew's cabin. Smoke came from the stone chimney at the side of the house.

"Looks like someone's home. We'll just wait in the car," Renee said, looking around.

"Aw, Mom," Justin said, rubbing the sleep from his eyes.

"Not on your life. You're part of this treasure hunt, too." Will led them up the steps to the front door. The log cabin had a porch running the full width of the house. Lawn furniture was covered with canvas tarps. An evergreen wreath hung on the front door. Will searched for a doorbell, then used the knocker beside the wreath.

They heard footsteps from within the cabin and then the door opened. Fred Askew looked at the trio standing there. "Yes?" he said.

"Are you Fred Askew?"

"None other."

"My name's Will Martin. I think you knew my grandfather."

A smile creased Fred's weather-worn face as he reached out and grabbed Will's hand. "So you're Will. Warren told me all about you. Come in, please. And who might this pretty lady be?"

"I'm sorry, this is Renee Carr, and her son," Will said.

"My name's Justin," said the boy.

Renee took the proffered hand. "I was Warren . . . Mr. Martin's secretary," she explained.

"We're sorry to come unannounced," Will began.

"Nonsense, get in here out of the cold."

The inside of the cabin smelled of wood smoke and pine. A Christmas tree stood in the corner and boxes of decorations were stacked on a table. A mounted deer head, a six-point buck, hung on the front of the stone chimney. A number of fishing rods were hung on the walls, and on one side of the chimney was a huge mounted German brown trout, on the other side a brilliantly colored brook trout. Justin immediately began inspecting the room.

"Justin," Renee said. "Don't touch a thing."

"Oh, he can't hurt nothin'," Fred said, waving his hand through the air.

"You two, have a seat on the couch. I'll clear away a spot on my bench."

Will and Renee sat down.

"Your granddad was my favorite customer. Every July he spent a week up here trolling the lake."

"I remember," Renee said. "He always had me block out a week on his calendar every year."

"I often thought of your grandfather as the brother I never had." The elderly man looked out the window. "Sometimes you don't realize how you're going to miss someone until he's gone."

"I know. I miss him, too," Will said.

"You ever do any fishing? You ought to come up and spend some time here. I remember your grandpa telling me what an athlete you were."

"Can I come?" Justin asked, tugging on Will's arm.

"Sure you can, young fella. Bring your mother along. Some of the old sailors thought women were bad luck. I've always found it the opposite!" The old man smiled. "Now, what can I do for you? I don't believe this is just a social call on an old man."

Will reached into his pocket and brought out the picture. "I found this in my grandfather's things. Do you remember when it was taken?" He handed Fred the photograph.

The old man studied the picture for a moment and his face lit up. "I'll never forget it. I think it was the first time the three of us went fishing together."

Will perked up. "Were there other times?"

"Many, many. That was another thing I liked about Warren. He never minded if I brought my wife along."

"Your wife?" Will asked, surprised.

"My sweet, sweet Lucy. I lost her last winter. Then Warren passed away. I lost my two best friends in one year. They were both one of a kind. It's been a tough year for me."

He wiped his eyes and handed the picture back to Will. "Why did you want to know about that particular trip?"

Will stared at the photograph, speechless.

Renee said, "Will's trying to put some pieces of a puzzle together, Mr. Askew. And this was one of the pieces."

Fred scratched his head through his thinning hair. "Glad to be of help."

Renee and Will stood up as Justin came scrambling over to their side. "Thanks for your time, Mr. Askew." Will shook the old man's hand.

"Thanks for visiting a lonely old man. Don't forget to come back," he nodded, as he let them out the door.

"I won't let them forget," Justin called over his shoulder.

Fred stood in the doorway of his cabin waving as they drove back down the country road.

"Lucy!" Will said. "I feel like such a fool. But in a way I'm relieved."

"Me, too," Renee said. "You almost had me losing faith."

"When are we going to come back?" Justin asked from the back seat.

"We'll have to see, sweetheart," said his mother.

"Ah, Mom. That's grown-up talk that means we won't come back." He yawned.

They drove in silence as night settled in around them.

"So where do you go now?" Renee whispered.

"I don't know." Will reached over and touched her hand as if it might bring him strength and courage.

"Have you found any other clues in the journals?"

Will sighed. "I've found a few names. But without exception they've either passed away or moved and left no forwarding address."

Renee snuggled down in the warmth of the seat. Her eyes were growing heavy. "If there's anything I can do, I'd be happy to help."

"Thanks. It looks like I'll need it. Here I was complaining about not wanting to wait until the last minute to get Gram her gift and there's only one week left until Christmas." Will looked over at Renee. "But I am going to get her what she wants, or die trying."

Renee's breathing slowed as her eyes closed.

As the miles flew by, Will's mind searched for any new clues as to the whereabouts of the elusive Lillian. At last they drove up to Renee's apartment. She awoke and stretched as Will stopped the car. "I haven't been very good company," she said.

Will opened the back door and lifted the sleeping Justin into his arms. He followed Renee up the stairs to her apartment and deposited the boy on his bed. Renee removed his shoes and pulled a blanket over him.

"I think he could sleep through an earthquake," Will said, as they returned to the living room. He noticed the roses were still in the center of the table.

"At least when he's asleep, he's quiet," Renee laughed.

Will grasped the doorknob. "Thanks for coming with me. There sure wasn't any gold at the end of that rainbow."

"I wouldn't be too sure about that," she replied. "You may find yourself with a new hobby come summer."

He laughed and nodded. "Anyway, you made it a pleasant drive."

"Thanks for asking us." As she patted his sleeve, her hand lingered on his arm. The two of them stared into each other's eyes for a moment before Will turned and walked down the steps to his car. Renee stood in the open doorway with her hands folded. As Will pulled away, she waved and he waved back.

19

I'LL BE BACK SHORTLY, MISS COOK," WILL SAID, AS HE PICKED UP HIS BRIEFCASE AND HEADED FOR THE DOOR. "I'M GOING OVER TO OUR LAWYER TO HAVE MR. JOBB WIT-ness some signatures." For the first time in weeks he smiled at Enid Cook. She flinched a bit, then the trace of a smile crossed her lips.

"That's fine, Mr. Martin."

"Oh, one more thing, Miss Cook. Could you please mail this photograph of my grandfather with Mr. and Mrs. Askew to Frederick Askew at Edenton Lake? Just jot a note saying I thought he'd enjoy having it, and send him my thanks and best wishes. The phone number is here, but directory assistance can probably give you the address."

Before Enid Cook responded, Will was out the door. He took a shortcut through the town park, as he tried to sift through the mixed emotions he had felt the previous day when he'd learned the woman in the photograph was Lucy Askew. He'd felt strangely relieved that Lillian still had no face, but he also felt a growing frustration with the lack of progress he was making. *Less than a week until Christmas and I still have no idea who Lillian is,* he thought. He had started past the gazebo that served as a bandstand during the summer months when he saw an old man lying on the bench. The man had newspapers pulled over him in a vain attempt to keep warm. Will started to take a different path, when the old man coughed violently and stretched a hand out toward him.

Will wavered for a moment, then turned back. "You look cold, old timer," he said.

The old man commenced a fit of coughing, then nodded his head. "Last night was real cold," he wheezed.

"I bet you could use some food to warm you up," Will said.

"I haven't had much to eat, lately," the old man shivered.

"Come with me." Will beckoned to the man to follow.

The old man rose creakily to his feet and neatly folded the newspapers, stowing them in a hiding spot beneath the gazebo. "Might need 'em tonight," he said, blowing on his hands to try to warm them. He was dressed in a dirty long-sleeved shirt and a pair of old wool pants. The cuffs of the pants were several inches above his shoe tops. He wore no stockings, and as he began to walk Will could hear the sole of one of the shoes slapping on the pavement. Will slipped off his overcoat and handed it to the old man.

"Put it on; you look like you need it worse than I do."

The man protested but let Will help him get into the coat. "You'll freeze," he said to Will.

"I don't have far to go. What's your name, friend?"

"Charlie Petersen."

"Mine's Will. Pleased to meet you."

"Let's get you over to Rosie's Cafe and get you something to eat, Charlie."

"Rosie don't like me much," the old man said. "Sometimes she catches me eating the food she's thrown out and she yells at me and chases me away."

Will led the old man into Rosie's and sat down at the table across from him.

"You don't have to do this, son," Charlie wheezed, as he pulled the coat closer around him. After a moment the ample woman who ran the cafe appeared at the table. She looked at the old man and her face hardened; then she noticed Will.

"Mr. Martin," she said. "What can I get for you?"

"Just a cup of hot chocolate for me, but I think you'd better bring my guest, Mr. Petersen, a platter of ham and eggs with hash browns and pancakes on the side. And a cup of steaming hot coffee." He looked at the old man. "Anything else?"

Charlie's eyes filled with tears. "That'll be fine."

Rosie lifted her nose and gazed at the old man. "Yes, Mr. Martin," she said, writing their order on a pad. She whirled around and headed to the kitchen.

Charlie stared at Will. "Why are you doing this, young man?"

Will shrugged his shoulders. "You looked like you needed help."

"I haven't always been like this, you know."

Will nodded. "I guess you never know when hard times might come your way."

Rosie returned with two steaming mugs. The old man warmed his hands around the cup and sipped the dark liquid. "Whoa, that's hot," he said, fanning his lips with one chapped hand.

Will blew into his cup of chocolate and gingerly took a sip. "That coffee will help warm you," he said. The two of them nursed their mugs until Rosie reappeared with a large platter of ham, eggs, and hash browns, which she placed in front of the old man. A second plate held a stack of pancakes. She snorted and left.

"Dig in," Will said.

"In just a minute." The old man closed his eyes, bowed his head, and mumbled a short prayer. When he had finished, he smiled at Will and then began to shovel the food into his mouth.

Will watched for a moment, then said, "Well, Charlie, I've got to get going. I was on my way to a meeting when our paths crossed." He reached into his wallet and pulled out fifty dollars. He handed it to the old man. "Get yourself something warmer to wear, including some thick socks."

"I can't take this from you," Charlie whispered. "Why would you do this?"

"Take it," Will said, "and merry Christmas. I'll pay Rosie on the way out."

The old man struggled to his feet. "Here. Take your coat." He began to remove Will's overcoat.

"You keep it until you get yourself a coat," Will said. "You can return it to me over at Martin Real Estate when you're through needing it."

"Martin Real Estate? You're not Warren Martin's grandson?"

"Yes . . . yes I am," Will said tentatively.

"No wonder you're a good man. Just like your grand-father."

"That's kind of you to say," Will replied.

"I'll return your overcoat shortly. God bless you, my son."

Will stopped at the cash register. "How much do I owe you, Rosie?"

She totaled the bill. "Five ninety-five," she said.

Will handed her a ten-dollar bill. "Keep the change."

"Thank you, Mr. Martin." She paused. "Could I ask you a question?"

"Sure."

She indicated the old man with her head. "How come you're helping old Charlie?"

"He looked like he needed help."

"You're starting to sound like your grandfather," she smiled.

"I guess worse things could happen," he said, as he left the cafe. He hurried down the sidewalk past two buildings and stopped at a third. He glanced at the gold leaf on the front door as he entered. DAVID JOBB, ATTORNEY AT LAW.

The outer office was finished in muted earth tones. Patricia Ames, David Jobb's secretary, sat behind her highly polished teak desk. "Mr. Martin," she enthused, "so good to see you. Go right in; Mr. Jobb is waiting for you."

Will smiled his thanks and pushed open the door into David Jobb's office. David sat behind his desk with his feet propped up on the edge of a potted plant. His half-moon eyeglasses were perched on the end of his nose. Although he was in his early sixties, his remaining fringe of hair was still jet black. He put down the brief he was reading and rose to greet his client. "Will, my boy. Good to see you." He removed his glasses and dangled them in his left hand while he extended his right hand to Will.

"Great to see you, too," Will said, shaking the older man's hand.

Jobb placed the spectacles in a pocket in his vest and gestured toward a chair. "Have a seat. What can I do for you?"

Will opened his briefcase and removed several documents. "I'd like you to look these over and, if you feel they're all right, I'd like you to witness my signature." He handed the pages to Jobb.

Jobb began to read the papers thoroughly. "This one seems fine," he said, and pushed it across the desk to his client. Will studied the office while Jobb read the rest of the papers. The walls were paneled in teak up to the chair rail. Above that was wallpaper in tan and gold vertical stripes. The top of the wall was finished with an ornate molding in cream and gold. The windows were draped with cream-colored fabric, which was pulled back with gold ties. The valence over the window was finished with a gold fringe. The office exuded an ancient elegance and warmth.

"They look fine, Will," Jobb said, handing them back to him. "Miss Ames is a notary public. We'll need to get her in here to do the notarizing and I'll witness." He pushed a button on his phone intercom and asked his secretary to join them.

Will signed each document, Patricia Ames stamped and signed as the notary, and David Jobb witnessed each signature. "Thank you, Mr. Jobb, Miss Ames," he said, as he placed the papers back in his briefcase.

"Any time we can be of assistance," Jobb said, rising from his desk. "That will be all for now, Miss Ames, thank you. Anything else I can help you with?"

Will closed his briefcase as Patricia Ames left the room, closing the door behind her. "Maybe one thing. Perhaps you could answer a question for me. You executed my grandfather's will, didn't you?" The lawyer nodded his head. "Who did he name as benefactors?"

"Well, now, I really can't answer that," Jobb smiled.

"Oh? Any reason?"

"Your grandfather wanted the will closed."

"Closed?" Will said. "Meaning what?"

"Well, of course you were named and I can tell you that, but I can't tell you the names of any of the others."

"What was his reason for doing that, Mr. Jobb?"

"Privacy, Will." The lawyer stroked his chin. "You have no idea how many people and charities will approach you if they know you have money," he concluded.

Will nodded. "Can you give me any hints?"

Jobb considered this for a moment. "Actually, several charities were included. Besides that, there are the two of you—that is, you and your grandmother. And one other individual."

Will straightened up and tried to keep his voice calm. "Just one other person?"

"Yes, one," Jobb said carefully.

"I don't want you violating a trust, Mr. Jobb, but just how much did he leave this person?"

Jobb stroked his chin again. "The person is well cared for. I don't believe I can say more." He smiled.

"I understand," Will said. "I don't suppose there would be any way of finding out her name?"

"Her name? What makes you think it's a woman? No. Even though I don't think it would hurt anything, I'm sorry, Will."

Will smiled. "I can see why my grandfather valued your service."

"Thank you. I hope you'll come to value it as well."

The lawyer shook Will's hand and led him to the door.

"Thanks again, Mr. Jobb—more than you know."

20

He strode back through the park to Martin Real Estate. There was no one near the gazebo. The day was clear and cold, and he thrust his hands into his trouser pockets to keep them warm. As he entered the office, he could feel a chill inside that was colder than any weather outside. Mrs. Harr was typing furiously. She barely acknowledged his greeting. He was walking toward his office when he heard loud voices coming from John Henning's office. He altered his course.

"You, Miss Cook, are just an accountant," Henning snarled. "I have no idea why you think you can tell me how to handle a real estate deal."

"I've been handling real estate since before you were born," she said reasonably.

"That may be the problem," he growled. "Maybe you've been handling things too long!"

"Good morning," Will said loudly. The two combatants whirled and stared at him. "John," he said in a flat tone, "could I see you for a minute?" He turned and left.

John arrived in Will's office a few paces behind him. "That woman is out of here!" he huffed, jabbing his thumb over his shoulder as they entered Will's office.

Will leaned back in his chair and placed his hand behind his neck. He smiled faintly at John Henning. "What's the problem, John?"

"The problem is that woman!" Henning slammed the door behind him. "I told Frank Payne to go over to Zach Perkins' place and tell him he had until tomorrow to come up with his back rent or he was out. He's two months behind! So old lady Cook hears about it and comes unglued."

"How come?" Will asked.

"Beats me! She says Perkins has been there for over thirty years and he has slow times just before Christmas, but when all his invoices come in, he catches up on the rent. Big deal! It's just part of the whole attitude around here. If the guy can't pay, he needs to go somewhere else. We're a business, not a soup kitchen."

"I understand," Will said.

"What's the matter with that old bird, anyway? She drives me up the wall."

"John, Enid was right when she said she'd been working here before you were born. Change is hard for her. It's hard for everybody. She just feels more comfortable with things staying the way they are."

"Why did you hire me?" Henning asked. "To make changes, right? To update this place."

"Of course, but maybe we don't need to move as quickly as we once thought."

"Can I speak frankly, Will? We're not going to be able to affect any changes as long as she's around. I think it's time we did a little housecleaning." He started for the door.

"John," Will stopped him. "One other thing. Before you make any major changes, run them past me, okay?"

Henning's face tightened. "Whatever you want. You're the boss." He stared into Will's face, then spun around and left.

Will turned to face the wall of citations and pictures. He studied the photographs for a moment. One of them was of Warren and Enid Cook. "Grandpa, I'm not sure you'll approve of the changes we're going to make. But I don't approve of Lillian." *Lillian! Who are you?* He stared at the nameplate Renee had placed on the credenza. Warren Martin's name stared back at him. Slowly he reached for the phone.

"Carr Dance Studio, can I help you?"

"Renee, it's Will. How about some lunch?"

"I only have an hour. Can you come over to BJ's? It's next to the shoe store."

"Sounds good to me. I've found out something interesting."

"Good. I can't wait to hear. Gotta go. See you in a few minutes."

Will hung up the phone and stared at his grandfather's name. After a moment, he emptied his briefcase and walked out to Janice Harr with a clutch of papers. "Have you got time to file these this afternoon?" he asked.

"Of course, Mr. Martin," she replied.

"Thank you. I'm going to lunch now," he said, heading out the door.

Renee was already seated at a booth when he entered BJ's. She waved and he slid in across from her.

"Sorry I made you hurry," she said, smiling.

"No worse than the rest of the morning," he replied cheerfully, picking up a menu.

"Fill me in."

"I walked into the office this morning to find John Henning and Enid Cook lacing up the gloves. No, that's wrong. I think they'd already gone two rounds before I got there. I'm getting tired of refereeing." He shook his head. "Maybe you ought to come to the next round."

"I'm afraid I wouldn't be an impartial judge."

"I suppose you'd be in Enid's corner."

"Especially after today," she said, pulling a letter from her purse.

"Oh?" Will said, raising an eyebrow.

"I just got this letter. It seems my rent will be going up nearly two hundred dollars a month beginning in January." Her eyes flashed.

"This came today?" Will looked confused.

Renee's voice softened. "You didn't know about this, did you?"

"No, of course not. But in all fairness, I probably share some of the blame. I'm the one who asked John to analyze our properties and bring them more in line with their market value."

"I'd say he's doing an excellent job," she said, with an edge to her voice.

"Probably," Will replied, as he looked at the table top. "I'm sorry, Renee."

"I caught you by surprise, didn't I," Renee said, more quietly.

Will looked out the window. "I went looking for someone who could guide us into the next century. You just take one look at Martin Real Estate and you know we're not up to speed with the rest of the industry. John Henning has impeccable credentials. He's a visionary. He sees the big picture." Will paused. "I just wish I were sure that his ideas are the right ones for Martin Real Estate."

"Will, there's no question I'm upset about the rent, but I'd tell you this whether my rent was involved or not. Treating people fairly is much more important than becoming a millionaire. The reason your grandfather was so successful was partly due to his ability to trust people. His handshake was his bond. I'm not saying some people didn't disappoint him, but for the most part they lived up to his expectations. When I started my business, I tried to run it the same way your grandfather ran his. And you know what? Not only do I have a good clientele, but I can look in the mirror and smile at the person I see there."

Will started to respond, but he was interrupted by the arrival of a waitress.

"Hi, Renee." The waitress sized up Will discreetly.

"Hello, Ann. This is my friend Will Martin."

"Pleased to meet you. Want the special and an ice tea?" Renee nodded her head.

"How about you?" she asked, jabbing her pen toward Will.

"Guess I'll have the same thing." He handed her his menu without looking at it.

"Two teas, two specials coming up." Ann pushed the pen back behind her ear and ripped the order from her pad. "Be here in a minute." She walked off toward the kitchen with the menus.

"I didn't mean to come down so hard, Will. Truce?"

"Truce," he agreed. "But since you brought up my grandfather, let me tell you what I found out this morning."

"What's that?" Renee asked, intrigued.

"I was over at David Jobb's law firm."

"And?"

"He told me that basically my grandpa's will had three beneficiaries: my grandmother, me, and a person he wouldn't name."

"A third person?"

Will nodded. "Suddenly it clicked."

"What clicked?"

"I started thinking about Grandpa's journals. Dozens of times he talks about how he loves children."

"So?"

"Lillian must be his child!"

"You've got to be kidding!"

"Listen, it makes sense. If Lillian were someone he'd had a relationship with, he wouldn't name her in his will. He wouldn't want anyone to know, not even his lawyer. But if she were a child, a child he had kept hidden from the rest of the world, he'd want to make certain she was cared for." Will's eyes sparkled with excitement.

Renee shook her head sadly. "Didn't you know your grandfather better than that? Honestly."

"I thought I knew him. But since I've started going through his journals I've learned all sorts of things that I never knew."

Renee sat shaking her head.

"Not that they're bad things. And as I read I find myself growing closer to him. It's really quite confusing. Sometimes it's almost as if he's speaking to me."

"And what does he say?" Renee asked, leaning across the table.

"I'm not sure. Every once in a while he just stops in the middle of a page and writes a line or two of scripture. The other day I was reading and suddenly he'd written, 'Father, forgive them, for they know not what they do.'"

"And what followed?" she asked.

"Nothing. The rest of the page was blank. No hint what led him to write that scripture."

They sat without speaking for a few moments.

"But what would ever lead you to believe he'd had a child with another woman, Will?"

"I don't know. I really am quite confused. But this morning, the idea just jumped into my head while I was at the law office. Suddenly it seemed to make sense. On the other hand, where would she have been all these years?"

Renee reached out and covered Will's hand with hers. "Will, I just can't believe your grandfather was unfaithful to your grandmother. Now, honestly, can you?"

"Okay, maybe it is far-fetched, but just go with me for a minute. What if there was just one time, a long time ago. I don't know what the circumstances were, but what if, just what if, he fathered a child. The man we knew and loved wouldn't desert her; he'd support her and her mother, find them somewhere to live. Not in this town, probably, but close enough. And once a year he'd invite his daughter here and he'd visit with her on Christmas Eve. He knew it would be safe because Gram and I would be out shopping."

"Oh, Will." Renee shook her head in disbelief.

A new thought occurred to him. "Renee, she was born in May. That's why the emerald pendant. It all fits."

"I think you're obsessed."

"Probably," he smiled weakly.

"I only worked for your grandfather for a short time, but I think I knew him better than you. Can't you just forget Lillian?"

Will shook his head. "Not now. Not when I'm this close."

"Here's your tuna salad," Ann said, placing a glass and a plate in front of each of them. "Enjoy."

21

THE WIND KEENED, SWIRLING SNOW AROUND THE HOUSE AS WILL AND HIS GRANDMOTHER PULLED INTO THE GARAGE. HE SPRANG FROM THE CAR AND OPENED THE door for her, before retrieving two sacks of groceries from the back seat.

"Thanks for the ride, dear," Ruth said, as they entered the kitchen.

"My pleasure." He set the bags of groceries on the counter and began putting them away.

"No, no. I can do that. You go rest," Ruth told him, taking the milk from his hands and opening the refrigerator door.

"You always did spoil me," he said, kissing her cheek and retreating to the living room with the day's paper. He looked at the Christmas decorations on the mantel. Pine boughs surrounded the mirror and large Christmas candles were arranged in the centers of halos of holly. Suddenly, his thoughts were of Christmases past when he and his grandmother had decorated the tree. His grandfather had always strung the lights with great care and precision and then the three of them had arranged the myriad ornaments. Will sank onto the sofa cushions and closed his eyes with the pleasure of remembering. Suddenly he remembered Lillian and the Christmas Eve visits, and the mood was broken.

Restless, he lit the candles, laid a fire for later, and returned to the kitchen. His grandmother was putting the last cans on the shelf in the pantry. "Gram, can I ask you a question . . . a personal one?"

"I don't see why not," she said, pausing and tucking a loose strand of hair in place.

"Why didn't you and Grandpa have more children?" Ruth straightened and looked quizzically at Will. "None of my business, of course," he added.

Ruth removed her coat and folded it over the back of a chair. "That's a fair question, Will. When our Samuel was born it was the greatest moment of our lives. We'd been married nearly five years and we were becoming concerned that something might be wrong, when I became pregnant. That next year the real estate business really began to boom. Warren was putting in long, long hours. Thankfully I didn't have to work, so I got to stay home and take care of Samuel. I think we both felt that our lives were full and complete. We never talked seriously about having more children."

Will nodded his head. His grandmother inspected his face, then took his hand and led him into the living room. They sat down on the sofa and stared straight ahead, lost in their separate thoughts.

"Are you thinking Lillian might be his child, Will?" Ruth asked, breaking the silence.

He looked at her with surprise, and then slowly nodded his head. "I'm not making this any easier, am I?"

She shook her head. "It had occurred to me, too. A father sees his child on Christmas Eve." She picked up her coat and walked to the hall closet and hung it up. Will followed her.

"What are you feeling, Gram? Are you angry?"

"Angry? No," she sighed. "Disappointed? Maybe."

"Gram, I'm afraid I am feeling angry—angry enough for both of us."

"Then I'm sorry I ever got you into this. I can tell that it's preying on you. And what's worse, I'm afraid it's changing the way you feel about your grandfather."

"Oh, Gram, it is and it isn't. Maybe I'm just frustrated. I read his journals and I find out things, wonderful things, that I never dreamed he had done. Ironically, through this experience, I've learned to appreciate him more than I ever did in life. On the other hand, there's this Lillian to contend with, whoever she is." He led his grandmother back to the couch. "Reading the journals and talking to people who knew Grandpa and my father has opened up a window to the world I probably never would have experienced any other way, so don't be sorry."

Ruth patted her grandson's hand. "Thank you, Will."

He stared out the window into the darkness. "It doesn't stop there. It's not just his journals. It seems like everyone I come in contact with has benefited from knowing Grandpa and has something good to say about him. It's almost like he's still here with us. Does that make any sense to you?"

A tear rolled down Ruth's cheek as she nodded. "Yes, it does." They sat in silence. "Will, you don't have to keep looking for Lillian. I don't need to know."

The wind whispered around the house as Will sat staring at the flickering candles on the mantel. "Oh yes I do, Gram. If not for you, for me."

She nodded and stood up. "Thank you for that lovely dinner, Will, and the trip to the grocery store. I think I'll go up to bed now." She touched his cheek and climbed the stairs to her room.

Will sat listening to the wind and smelling the aroma of pine. Memories flooded over him again. The house grew quiet and he stood up and walked to the office. He turned on the desk lamp and walked softly around the room. Every picture, every knickknack on the shelf was a reminder of happier times. The wind suddenly squealed at the window-pane and Will hugged himself involuntarily. He thought back to the old man in the town square and wondered if he'd ever see his overcoat again.

Will turned out the light and walked to the hall closet. In the dim light from the living room, he opened the door and removed his grandfather's coat. As he slid his arms into the overcoat he could smell the scent that clung to the fab-ric. The coat was only slightly too large. On a whim, he removed his grandfather's hat from the shelf in the closet and placed it on his head. It fit perfectly. He turned, with a smile on his face, and saw his reflection in the front door window.

Still wearing the coat and hat, Will returned to the office and removed a picture of his grandfather from the wall next to the fireplace. The photograph had been taken at his father's sixth birthday party. He returned to the foyer and compared his image with that of the man in the picture. The resemblance was so uncanny it sent chills up his spine. Then a warm glow spread through his body. Will returned the picture to its place and walked softly to the foyer, where he hung up the coat and hat. He smiled as he blew out the candles, turned off the living room light, and climbed the stairs to his bedroom.

He sat down at his desk and opened one of the journals. Quickly he scanned the pages, stopping only to write down a name here and there that sounded promising. By midnight a half-dozen new leads had been written down on the pad. Wearily, he climbed into bed.

22

Will sat in the swivel chair staring out the window at the park. He held the phone with his shoulder. "I understand, Mr. Phillips. I'm sorry to have bothered you. Good-bye." He swiveled around and placed the phone back on its cradle. He removed the pen from the desk set and crossed off the last name on the list he had created the previous night. The phone rang.

"Merry Christmas. Martin Real Estate, how may I help you?"

"Will, is that you?" The voice on the other end of the line was his boss from his other job, his other life.

"Yes, Mr. Cauley, it is."

"I'm just calling to make sure you'll be back here in New York the first week in January."

"I was going to call you later today, Mr. Cauley. I might need another month's extension."

"What! I think you've had long enough. We need you back here."

Will took a deep breath. "I've discovered the agency's in worse shape than I thought."

"What did I tell you? Sell it. Get what you can for it, then get back here."

"I think I can get things turned around by the first of February."

"Don't be foolish. We've given you months. If you're not in your office by January fifteenth, then you don't need to worry about coming back! Do you understand?"

Will pivoted in his chair and looked out at the square.

"Do you understand?" Cauley's voice crackled over the wire.

"Absolutely, sir."

"Then, we'll see you next month," Cauley barked, and then, as an afterthought, "and merry Christmas."

"Merry Christmas to you," Will replied, turning to hang up the phone. He turned back to the vision of the park and was thinking about his life on Wall Street when he heard a knock. "Come in," he called, as he turned around to see Enid Cook at his door.

"I'm sorry to disturb you, Mr. Martin, but these need to be signed."

Will took the checks and signed each one. Nervously, Enid shifted her weight slowly from one foot to the other.

"Mr. Martin, I'm sorry about that little tiff with Mr. Henning. I don't know why I let him get to me. It wasn't my place to speak about the Perkins account."

"Yes it was," Will said, as he handed the checks back to Miss Cook. "Of course it was."

Her jaw dropped as she took the pieces of paper from him. "What?"

"You had every right to express your opinion." Will smiled at her and she turned to go.

"Miss Cook," he said. "May I ask you a question?"

"Of course, Mr. Martin." She turned back to his desk.

Will looked out the window. "This may seem strange, but, you worked for my grandfather for many years."

"Yes, Mr. Martin."

"Was there ever a time when he mentioned anyone named Lillian?"

She stood silently looking at the back of Will's head. "Miss Cook? I'd really like to know."

"I wish I could be of some help, Mr. Martin, but I'm sorry. I never heard him mention anyone by that name."

"I'm sorry, too."

She turned to leave. Then, puzzled by the question, she turned back. "Mr. Martin?"

"Yes."

"Is it important?"

"I think it's very important, Miss Cook."

"I see." Enid Cook backed out of the office and closed the door.

The rest of the day was amazingly busy for December twenty-third. Before Will knew it, darkness began to settle on the town and the Christmas lights came winking on. There was a knock on Will's door. "Come in."

John Henning stuck his head in the office. "Just thought I'd tell you I'm leaving for the day," he said gruffly.

"Good night, John," Will replied.

Henning stepped into the room. "Oh, by the way, someone came by earlier and left this for you." He placed Will's overcoat on the coat rack and walked away.

Will stared with disbelief, and then a smile crossed his face. He turned back to the work before him. An hour passed, then two. The stacks of papers on his desk were considerably smaller. Only Henning's report lay untouched. He leaned back in the chair and opened the volume, but before he could begin reading he was interrupted by the sound of carolers outside the window. He closed the book, gathered his coat, and turned out the light.

He drove slowly around the town square. Tiny lights

sparkled from the branches of the huge maples. An enormous pine tree on the edge of the square had been decorated with thousands of lights. *Better than Rockefeller Center,* he thought, as he stopped at a red light. Shoppers hurried across the street, many laughing and talking. Will's gaze followed them to the sidewalk in front of the building his grandfather had first purchased. It stood majestically, looking down on the square. A horn sounded. The light had turned green. Will pulled the Jaguar to the curb and parked it.

"Merry Christmas!" called the street-corner Santa Claus in front of Christensen's Department Store. Will pulled the overcoat tightly around him. He walked through the chill of the winter night down Main Street. The stores were filled with throngs of people completing their Christmas shopping. He felt as if he had come home.

He found himself directly across the square from where he'd parked his car. The carolers had strolled to the gazebo where he had found the old man the day before. "Charlie," he whispered. "That was his name." He stopped to listen to the carolers.

"Angels we have heard on high . . ."

His breath formed ghostly clouds, and the cold stung his ears and the tip of his nose. He plunged his hands into the pockets of his coat to keep them warm. He felt a piece of paper in the right-hand pocket. A small crowd had formed around him, listening to the carolers.

"God rest ye merry, gentlemen, . . ." they began singing softly.

Will made his way across the square to his car. He unlocked it and pulled the paper from his pocket as he seated himself. It was a small envelope. He opened it and inside was a fifty-dollar bill and a penciled note. *Thank you, my brother,* was all it said. Will glanced back toward the gazebo, then drove slowly home.

He could smell the yeasty aroma of freshly baked bread as he entered the kitchen. He smiled as he walked to the hall closet and hung up his coat. His grandmother was dozing in her rocking chair at the side of the fireplace. As he closed the door her eyelids opened. "Will, I was worried about you."

"I'm sorry, Gram. Still, you're just going to have to get used to the fact I'm thirty-two," he smiled.

"It's just that I have something I need to say to you before I can go to bed." She rose from the rocking chair and took his hands. "Come sit here with me," she said, leading him to the sofa. The two of them sat facing each other. "Ever since we talked last night, I've felt that I've been unfair to you." She shifted on the couch and looked toward the fireplace. "I've sent you off looking for someone who is just a will-o'-the-wisp from the past. Whatever relationship she and Warren had is long past and certainly won't be changed through our efforts. Your grandfather and I had a wonderful long life together. There is nothing that is going to change what we had and how I feel about him. And no specter from the past is going to change the love the two of us felt for each other. I'm not sure he did anything that needs forgiveness, but if there is something, then I forgive him."

Will smiled at his grandmother. "Funny you should say that, Gram. Just the other day I read a passage about forgiveness in one of his journals."

"Maybe we're even closer than I thought."

"Maybe you are. Maybe we all are." He stood to leave.

"I left a journal on your bed. I've marked a passage I want you to read."

"Thanks, Gram." He leaned and kissed her on the cheek. "Anything to do with Lillian?"

"No. Something more important."

"Oh?" said Will. "I'd better go read it." He climbed the stairs to his room. The journal lay on his bed with a gold bookmark sticking from the top of it. Will picked up the book and sat down at his desk. He opened to the marked page.

It is Will's sixteenth birthday today. He has turned into such a fine young man. I have marveled at his talent and how he has grown in wisdom and in stature and in favor with God and man. I'm not very good at telling him how much I love him. I hope he knows it. I try to support him in all he does. The years have slipped by and we have become easier with each other, closer. Oh, Will, you are truly my son. No father could be prouder than I. I wish you knew how you have filled the void in my heart.

Tears formed in Will's eyes as he closed the book. He stared blankly out the window into the frosty night, fighting back a lump in his throat. As he went to place the book on the desk he spied a small slip of paper sticking out of the bottom of the journal. He opened to that page.

This afternoon we visited José Rivera and picked out our Christmas tree. It's a strange custom we have, waiting till the last moment. But it does ensure that the tree is fresh. I can hardly wait to decorate it.

Will closed the book. *Tomorrow we continue the tradition,* he said to himself. He glanced at his watch. Nearly ten o'clock. He picked up the phone.

"Hello."

"Hello, Renee. This is Will."

"I hope this isn't going to become a habit," she laughed softly. "It's awfully late."

"Later than you think. Listen, I've called to offer you two invitations."

"Invitations?"

"Are you teaching tomorrow?"

"On Christmas Eve? You've got to be kidding."

"Good! How would you and Justin like to go with me to pick out a Christmas tree? I found a new name to add to my Lillian list. José Rivera. He runs a tree farm out near Maple Hills."

"You do leave things to the last minute, don't you?" Renee replied, but there was excitement in her voice. "We'd love to go."

"I hoped you'd say that." Will smiled.

"What's the second invitation?"

"The office party is tomorrow morning. I think it would be great if you and Justin could come."

"Oh, Will, I don't . . ."

"Renee?"

"It's been ten years since I started the dance studio. Are you sure you want me there?"

"Absolutely. Both you and Justin."

"Well, then I suppose it would be all right."

"Great! I'll see you at nine in the morning."

"Nine?"

"We're going to have a Christmas brunch and then let everyone go home early."

23

Enid Cook sat primly at her desk. The agents were just beginning to arrive. She heard the door to Will's office open.

"Miss Cook?" he whispered. "Have you made out the bonus checks?"

"Of course," she said quietly.

"Would you give them to me please? I'd like to hand them out, just as my grandfather did."

"Oh?" She opened her desk drawer and withdrew the neat stack of envelopes. "Sometimes you surprise me," she said.

"I hope so, Miss Cook," he said, as he returned to his office.

Will put the stack of envelopes behind his grandfather's nameplate and leaned them against the wall. He ran his finger over the engraved brass plaque. "Here we go, Grandpa," he said to himself. He walked quickly to John Henning's office.

"You're here early," said Henning, rising from behind his desk. "The secret's not a secret anymore."

"What secret?" asked Will.

"The building across the square. I think Sterling Conrad tipped Hunter Hoggard off. The bidding war's beginning. I think we can get top price for it. It will be the first, but not the last, sale of the new year!"

"We're not going to sell it," Will said flatly.

"What do you mean?" Henning's voice rose. "There's no way we can afford to renovate it and make a profit. This is a great chance to unload it."

"John, I don't think you're going to understand, but that building was the first one my grandfather ever bought."

"So?"

"So, it's not for sale."

"Will, quit making decisions with your heart. Use your head!" Henning leaned forward with both hands on his desktop.

Will nodded his head. "John, if this were a month ago, I'd probably agree with you. But," Will stopped and cleared his throat, "things have changed."

"And I thought that's what you brought me in to do. Make things change. What's going on here?" Henning asked, his voice rising another notch.

Will inhaled and held his breath for a moment. Then he said, "John, you're a good man. You've got great qualifications. But, I don't think you're really ever going to be happy working for Martin Real Estate." He withdrew an envelope from his jacket.

"Here's two months' severance pay." He handed the envelope to Henning.

"You're firing me on Christmas Eve?" Henning shook his head in disbelief as he took the envelope. "I can't believe this."

"John, I'm freeing you. You're young and smart and amply qualified. I'm giving you a chance to find a job where you'll be happy. I don't think you ever will be here."

"What about our plan? You and I were going to take this town by storm. Get rich."

"Plans change, John. So do people." Will turned to leave. "You'll be fine. I know you will. Thank you for everything you did for Martin Real Estate while you were here."

"And what will happen to you?" he asked. "You and this agency?"

"We'll be fine, too." He walked out Henning's door.

John Henning ripped open the envelope and looked at the check inside. The sum was twice what he'd expected. He smiled a thin smile and shrugged his shoulders. He opened the drawers of his desk and placed a few items in his brief-case. Then he reached behind him to remove a couple of framed awards from the wall. Those fit in his briefcase as well. He put on his coat and, without a backward glance, walked out the front door of Martin's Real Estate, nearly bumping into the first of the caterers to arrive with the food for the office party.

Will returned to his office and retrieved the bonus checks, which he stuck in his coat pocket.

By nine o'clock the buffet had been set up and Christmas music filled the office. Ruth Martin opened the front door and entered the room. Will spotted his grandmother and smiled. "Perfect timing! The life of the party has arrived," he said, walking over and kissing her on her cheek.

"It doesn't look like it needs me," said Ruth, smiling as she looked around at the people talking, eating, and exchanging gifts.

"Oh, but it does," Will said, laughing. "How does the place look, Gram? It's been a while since you visited."

Ruth surveyed the office. "Perfect."

"Excuse me," Renee said, as she pushed the door open, nearly hitting Will from behind.

"Renee!" he chortled. "Do you remember my grand-mother?"

"Of course!" Renee gave Ruth a hug. "Mrs. Martin, you're looking well."

"Thank you, dear. You look as though you're prospering in the world of dance."

Will knelt down. "And this, Gram, is Renee's son, Justin. Justin, this is my grandmother."

Gram reached out and took Justin's hand. "I'm pleased to meet you, young man," she said.

"Will knows lots about dinosaurs," the boy said proudly.

"Oh, he always loved dinosaurs when he was a boy. Just like you, I'd guess."

Justin smiled and nodded.

"Now that everyone's here, I want to make an announcement," Will said, rubbing his hands together.

Ruth and Renee looked at each other quizzically, as Will walked over to Enid Cook's desk. Carefully he moved her folders and papers aside and jumped up on the desk. "Could I have your attention, please," he called over the sound of the Christmas carols coming from the CD player on Janice Harr's desk.

The entire office staff stared in amazement. Janice reached over and switched off the music. The room became deathly quiet.

Will withdrew the stack of bonus-check envelopes from his suitcoat pocket. "I'm sure I have something here you'd all like to have." A murmur of agreement went through the office. "I appreciate the support you've given me over these past few months. I'm sure you've wondered where we were going. My grandfather founded this agency half a century ago and he turned it into one of the most respected businesses in town."

Heads nodded in agreement.

"When my father was old enough, he joined the agency. Everyone tells me he and my grandfather shared the same philosophy. If it had not been for an unfortunate accident, he would undoubtedly be here today, instead of me."

All eyes were on Will.

"But that isn't the way things worked out. When Grandpa died, he left me the agency. I was living in New York, as you all know, and I'd been lucky enough to get a job at one of the most prestigious firms on Wall Street. Long before I deserved to be, I'd become the youngest member of the firm ever to become a vice president. The rewards were enormous even if the hours were long. Quite frankly, I didn't want to come home. Martin Real Estate was a pothole in the highway of my life."

The real estate agents looked at one another. Ruth reached out and took Renee's hand.

"But in the past few months, things have changed." Another murmur went through the crowd. "More accurately, I've changed. Martin Real Estate has changed from a pothole to a freeway. What I'm trying to say in this roundabout way is that I'm not going back to New York."

Renee squeezed Ruth's hand.

"It took my grandfather's death to bring me home. The least I can do is try not to make him ashamed of me. There have been rumors of changes in the way we do business, but I've decided if they were good enough for two generations of Martins, they're good enough for three. Today, I thanked John Henning for the assistance he gave us over the past difficult months and bade him adieu."

A ripple of amazement spread among the agents.

"I'm not perfect and I have a lot to learn. I'm hoping you have enough patience and forgiveness to teach me." Will looked at Renee. She smiled. "Thank you. And merry Christmas."

Will hopped down from the desk and began sorting through the bonus envelopes. Slowly Enid Cook began to applaud, and by the time Will had reached his grandmother's side, the entire staff was applauding loudly. His grandmother hugged him. "Merry Christmas, Will. Welcome home."

Will began making his way among the agents, handing each an envelope. The music was turned back on and the noise level in the room rose rapidly. After a few minutes he found himself standing by Justin and Renee. She beckoned to him. He leaned down to hear what she wanted to say, and she touched his cheek and kissed him lightly on the mouth.

"Will, you've given your grandmother the best Christmas gift she could ever have. I don't think you need to find Lillian."

"Oh, but I do, Renee. I need to find her. For me." He hugged her close. "Let's go get a Christmas tree."

Will waved good-bye to his grandmother, who was surrounded by old friends, and he, Renee, and Justin slipped out the front door.

24

THE JAGUAR SPED THROUGH THE BRIGHT
CHRISTMAS EVE MORNING TOWARD MAPLE
HILLS. "WHERE ARE WE GOING, WILL?"
JUSTIN ASKED.

"To get a big Christmas tree," Will replied.

"How come you don't have one already?"

"It's a Christmas tradition in my family. We always got
our tree on Christmas Eve." Will smiled as they hummed
down the highway. Ten minutes later they pulled into
Rivera's Tree Farm.

"Do you want to pick out our tree?" Will asked Justin.

The little boy looked at the forest of green. "Sure! But they all look good to me," he said.

"It looks like the big ones are out there," Will said, pointing down a path between the trees.

"I'll go see," Justin yelped, as he started running down the path.

Will and Renee walked to a small shed with a hand-lettered sign. RIVERA'S TREES, FRESH FROM THE FOREST.

A man dressed in a down parka and a plaid cap with earflaps was helping tie down the back door of a minivan. Pine branches stuck out through the partly open hatch. "Might be better to put it on top," he said to the driver. "That way you don't get exhaust fumes into the car." A few minutes later he had secured the tree to the top of the van with heavy twine.

"Can I help you folks?" he asked, turning to Will and Renee.

"I don't know if you remember me or not, Mr. Rivera, but I'm Will Martin. My grandfather, Warren Martin, and I used to get our tree here every year." José's face split with a grin. He reached out with both gloved hands and grabbed Will's hand. "Well, I didn't even recognize you. I'm so glad to see you."

"Thank you, José."

"Christmas Eve. Time to get your grandfather's tree."

"Yes."

"I was afraid you weren't coming. Most of the really good trees are gone."

"Oh, it looks as if you still have plenty," Will chuckled.

"Well," José smiled mischievously, "your grandfather used to come out at least three weeks before Christmas to pick out a tree. Then when Christmas Eve came around he knew a fine-looking tree was waiting for him. When no one came this year I thought I'd better pick one out for you myself." He indicated with a toss of his head. "It's behind the shed. Has your grandmother's name on it."

"Thank you, José. I really appreciate your taking care of us this way."

"No problem. After all, your grandfather was the reason I'm here."

"I didn't know that," Will said.

José sucked on his bottom lip. "Yep. Your grandpa owned this piece of land." He indicated the huge expanse of trees and fields with his hands. "Offered it to me at a fair price. After I went to every bank in town and got turned down for a mortgage, he sold it to me on contract and let me make the payments directly to him. Just on the shake of a hand. He was one of a kind."

"So I'm learning."

Justin came scampering down the path. "The best tree," he said breathlessly, "is one right back here." He tugged on Will's hand. José followed the three of them around the shed to the tree he had tagged for the Martins.

"You know your trees, young man," José said, smiling.

Will reached out and put his hands on José's arm. "José, can I ask you a question?"

"Sure."

"I'm looking for a friend of my grandfather's. A woman named Lillian. Did he ever mention that name to you?"

José removed the cap from his head and smoothed his hair. "No. I don't think so. The only woman he ever mentioned was his Ruth. Used to say he needed the most perfect tree for the most perfect woman. Just Ruth." He shoved the cap back on his head. "Sorry, Mr. Martin."

"That's okay," Will said.

"Do you want me to deliver this tree?" José asked.

Will looked at the size of the tree and his car. "I'd appreciate it, José." He pulled out his wallet. "How much do I owe you?"

"Do you want me to deliver the other one, too?"

"What other one?" Will asked. Renee grabbed his arm and a chill went through him.

"The ten-footer for Martha Fields. Your grandfather always sent a tree each year."

"Martha Fields?" Will got a cold feeling in the pit of his stomach. "Where does she live?"

"I don't have the address in my head, but I think I have it written down in my order book."

"If it's not too much trouble," Will said, as José headed for the shed.

Will turned to Renee. "Lillian, now Martha."

"Will," she said, shaking her head.

He threw his hands in the air. "At some point you're going to have to believe the evidence. Do you think this is another coincidence?"

"Yes," Renee said. "I believe it is."

"Renee, I'm really not trying to shake your faith in Grandpa, but this is getting worse and worse."

José returned. "The address is seventy-eight hundred Beverly Way. Do you want me to deliver a tree?"

"Yes," Renee said. "Will, pay the man."

José looked uncertain. "It's forty dollars for the two trees," he said.

Will pulled out his wallet and withdrew the fifty-dollar bill that had been returned to him. "Merry Christmas, José. Keep the change," he said, as he followed Renee and Justin to the car.

The three of them drove back into town in total silence. Will pulled up in front of Renee's apartment. "See you tonight, Will?" she asked, as the car came to a halt. Justin hopped out the back door and ran up the steps.

Will reached over and took Renee's hand. "I've been thinking. When Gram asked me to find Lillian, it was like a puzzle that needed to be solved. When you work on Wall Street that's what you do. You make predictions, you solve things. I'm pretty good at it."

She nodded her head.

"Renee, this has taken on a life of its own. As much as I want to find out who Lillian is, I don't want to find that she's some shady woman from my grandfather's past. I don't want to discover she's his daughter, either. But I do want to solve the puzzle. You know that, don't you?"

She reached out and patted his cheek. "Of course, Will."

He pulled her closer and kissed her. "Thanks for understanding." He kissed her again, more fervently. "Until tonight."

Renee slid out of the car and raced up the steps to let Justin into their apartment.

25

WILL SAT IN FRONT OF RENEE'S APARTMENT FOR A FEW MINUTES. THE CONFUSION OF THE PAST WEEKS RUMBLED IN HIS MIND. *LILLIAN, YOU'RE NO CLOSER NOW THAN YOU were at the beginning of this mess,* he thought. *Seventy-eight hundred Beverly Way!* He might not know who Lillian was, but at least he had the address of Martha Fields, whoever she was. But did he really want to know who she was? *Oh, Grandpa, why couldn't your life have been simpler?*

Will shifted into gear and decided to return home, but two blocks down the road his curiosity got the best of him. He made a quick turn at the corner and headed toward Martha's address. The blocks flew by until he climbed a hill on the outskirts of town and found himself on Beverly Way. As he approached the address he'd been given, he saw a long driveway leading to a sprawling brick building. A sign at the bottom of the driveway said, MARTHA FIELDS NURSING HOME. Will eased the Jaguar up the drive.

He climbed the wide sandstone steps, somewhat embarrassed. *Grandpa, why do I always assume the worst?* He opened the front door and entered the reception area. To his right was a sun room, and a number of the nursing-home residents were there surrounded by visiting families. Will wandered slowly down the hallway to his left.

"Is there something I can do to help you?" an authoritative voice rang out.

Will turned to see a woman in her mid-fifties dressed in a severe gray suit.

"I don't know," he blurted out. "It's a little hard to explain."

"I'm the manager," said the woman, extending her hand. "I'm Mrs. Baker. I'm in charge of the Martha Fields Home."

Will took her hand. "I'm Will Martin—"

"Warren Martin's grandson!" she finished the sentence for him.

"Yes. But how . . . ?"

Mrs. Baker looked thoughtful. "You look just like a younger version of him."

"So I've been told." Will smiled.

She nodded her head. "Well, it's very nice to meet you face to face."

"I'm sorry about the Christmas tree. I didn't find out about it until this morning. It will be delivered shortly. I hope it's not too late?"

"No, no, no. That will be perfect. What better night to decorate a Christmas tree than Christmas Eve. It would please your grandfather to continue the tradition."

"I think you're right, Mrs. Baker."

"We always waited until Christmas Eve to decorate the tree. Your grandfather used to come place a few of the ornaments himself while he was visiting."

"I didn't know that."

"He was such a busy man and yet he took the time to visit every patient in our home."

"It sounds just like him."

"And then he'd always go spend some time with Lillian."

Will's heart leapt in his chest. "Lillian?" He reached out and grabbed both of Mrs. Baker's hands.

"Lillian," Mrs. Baker nodded. "He was her only visitor, you know. She's been here the past twenty-eight years, and no one else ever came to visit her. Your grandfather was regular as clockwork. He dropped in at least once a month to check on her, and then on Christmas Eve he spent an hour or so with her. She slipped into a coma several years ago, but he kept up his vigil.

"Mrs. Baker," Will asked huskily. "May I see her?"

"Of course. She's in such poor health now. I'm surprised she outlived your grandfather." Mrs. Baker led Will down the hallway to the last room. It was painted pale pink and had lace curtains at the window.

Will looked at the frail, white-haired woman lying in her hospital bed. Her cottony hair was neatly combed. Her hands lay beside her, the talon-like fingers grasping an imaginary object. Her eyes stared sightlessly at the ceiling. Her mouth was an open black oval.

"What connection did my grandfather have with her?" Will asked.

"I'm really not sure. I began managing the home just a few weeks before she got like this. She's the longest surviving patient in our care. Apparently she fell asleep at the wheel of her car and crashed into another one, killing the young couple in it and paralyzing herself from the waist down."

Slowly Will's head turned. "How long did you say she's been here?"

"Just over twenty-eight years."

"Ever since the automobile accident?"

"Yes," Mrs. Baker nodded.

Will looked back at Lillian and tears filled his eyes.

"Mr. Martin, what's wrong?"

Will wiped the tears away with his hand.

"Mr. Martin?"

"I'll be fine, Mrs. Baker, just fine."

"You know, Mr. Martin. There are a lot worse things than death." She gestured toward Lillian.

"Yes there are. Many things."

26

Justin bounced in the back seat as Will and Renee pulled into the garage. The scent of pine enveloped them as they entered the kitchen door. "That's one reason to wait until Christmas Eve to put up the tree," Will said, taking a deep breath. The three of them entered the living room. Will had put the lights on the tree before he had left to pick up Renee and Justin, and Ruth was beginning to place ornaments on the tree.

"Merry Christmas," Renee called out, as they entered the room.

"Merry Christmas, to you," Ruth replied, coming over to greet them.

They set about putting the rest of the ornaments on the tree; then Will began bringing out gaily wrapped packages to place under it.

"Can I help?" Justin asked, too excited to keep still.

"Sure," Will said. The two of them carried out several more gifts.

"Hey," Justin said. "This one says 'to Justin from Will.' " He began to shake it. The package made an intriguing rattle.

"You can open it if you want," Will said, tousling the boy's sandy hair.

The wrapping paper turned to confetti as Justin ripped open the box. He poured out an assortment of detailed plastic dinosaurs and the skeleton of a tyrannosaurus.

"Wow, a Stegosaurus," Justin said, as he picked up one of the dinosaurs. He ran to Will and gave him a big hug.

"I hope you don't mind if they're used. I don't have much need for my collection anymore."

"Is this a new tradition or an old one—opening gifts on Christmas Eve?" Renee asked. She reached into her purse and handed Will a package wrapped in scarlet red foil.

He opened it carefully and slid out a brass nameplate, identical to the one at work except this one said, WILL MARTIN. The lights from the tree reflected rainbow colors across the polished surface.

"Is it okay?" Renee asked hopefully.

"Perfect," he said, staring at his reflection in the shiny brass.

"Can I hand out the others?" Justin asked.

"Might as well," Will said, smiling.

Quickly the boy looked at the name tags. "Here's one for you," he said, handing Ruth a small gold-wrapped gift.

Ruth untied the scarlet bow and removed the wrapping paper. She opened the velvet box to reveal the emerald pendant. "Oh, Will. You shouldn't have," she cried.

"I didn't," he stammered. "Grandpa had Mr. Taylor make it for you. He picked out the stone some time before he died."

Her lips began to tremble and tears streamed down her face. "Thank you, Will. Thank you."

"You're welcome. But I'm confused, Gram. An emerald isn't your birthstone."

"No, Will, it isn't. But it's the birthstone for May, the month your grandfather and I met. He always said that our meeting was a rebirth for both of us."

Renee cleared her throat and smiled at Will.

"Actually, I do have a gift for you, Gram. But you'll have to come with me to get it."

"Oh?"

"Trust me," Will said.

The four of them bundled up against the winter cold and climbed into Will's car.

"What's this all about?" Gram asked, as they cruised down the street.

"Don't you know better than to ask about a Christmas gift, Gram?"

They pulled up the long drive to the Martha Fields Nursing Home. Renee cocked an eyebrow as she recognized the name. Will just smiled an enigmatic smile. He led them up the steps to the foyer. A large Christmas tree had been centered in the sun room, and patients and their families were placing ornaments on it.

"I think we need to go put an ornament on the tree," Will said. The four of them entered the sun room. While the others joined in the hanging of ornaments, Will placed his ball on the tree and left quickly to find Mrs. Baker. In a moment he returned and said to his three companions, "This way." He led them down the hall to an open door. Renee and Justin stood in the doorway as Will led his grandmother to Lillian's bed.

He put his arm around her and whispered, "This is the poor woman who had the terrible misfortune of being behind the wheel of a car and too tired to keep her eyes open twenty-eight years ago."

Ruth's forehead puckered for a moment; then a flood of recognition came over her. She turned to Will questioningly.

"Yes, Gram. It's Lillian. Merry Christmas." He hugged his grandmother.

Ruth sank into the chair at Lillian's side. "Oh, Warren." Tears coursed down her cheeks. "Lillian."

"He forgave her, didn't he, Gram."

She nodded her head. "Blessed be the peacemakers," she whispered, as she hugged her grandson tightly.

"Gram, this has been both the most frustrating and the most rewarding month of my life. I've learned more about Grandpa than I ever learned in the years we lived together. I'm not sure whether this is your Christmas gift, or mine. But thank you for sending me on this quest."

Ruth reached out and took Lillian's hand in her own and began to stroke it gently. "Will, I think I'll stay here for a while."

The sound of carols floated softly into the room. Will left his grandmother's side and walked toward the sun room with Renee and Justin. Renee slipped her arm around Will and hugged him gently.

"Seems like you're the only one who hasn't had a Christmas gift," he said, as they reached the doorway of the sun room. He slipped his hand into his pocket and pulled out a small jewelry box. He handed it to Renee. She opened it slowly. The diamond ring sparkled in the Christmas lights.

"Oh, Will! Are you sure?"

"If you are," he replied. Slowly she nodded her head.

He took her in his arms. Justin smiled approvingly, then turned his attention to a platter of cookies. In the sun room the patients and their families were sitting around the brightly lit Christmas tree, singing softly. Will and Renee joined in.

Silent night, holy night
All is calm, all is bright
'Round yon virgin mother and child
Holy infant so tender and mild
Sleep in heavenly peace . . .

Down the hall, Ruth stroked Lillian's hand and gently repeated, "Sleep in heavenly peace."

ABOUT THE AUTHOR

RICHARD SIDDOWAY is a Utah State legislator and an educator in the Utah public school system. He is the author of three previous books.